C000246413

Same World, Different Story

Chapter One

2010

Kaitlyn was abruptly woken from her dreams by the sound of her mum and dad's urgent whispering somewhere nearby.

She blinked open her eyes to find them both standing over her bed with their heads bent together as they discussed something that they both seemed quite distressed by.

"What's going on?" Kaitlyn asked as she groggily pulled herself up to a seated position. Looking at the clock beside her bed she saw that it was 10am meaning she'd slept later than she had intended, but she still didn't think a bit of a lie in on a Saturday warranted being woken up by her parents.

Her mum and dad both turned to look at her once they'd realised she was awake, and she was taken aback by the worry in their eyes.

Something must have happened.

She braced herself for bad news so was confused when her mum only said, "You're not going to Ellis's house this afternoon to do your homework. You can do it here, by yourself."

Kaitlyn frowned. "Why? We always do our homework together. He helps me with science. Did he call to cancel?"

Her mum shook her head. "No, I'm cancelling. In fact, I don't want you hanging around with Ellis anymore. He isn't good company to keep."

She left the room without any further explanation, with Kaitlyn's dad trailing behind her having not said a single word.

Kaitlyn chased after them both. "What's going on? Why can't I be friends with Ellis anymore? Did you fall out with his mum?"

Kaitlyn's mum had been best friends with Ellis's since they were both teenagers and it had meant that their children had grown up close as well.

Ellis was her best friend. They did everything together. She couldn't imagine why her mum could have changed her mind about him.

"No, it's his brother that's the problem," her mum said, still being vague.

"Nicholas? Why? What did he do?"

At that point her mum looked at her dad, beseeching him with her eyes to explain for her, as if the words were too difficult for her to say.

Kaitlyn met her dad's serious gaze and blank expression, dreading whatever he might be about to tell her.

"Nicholas was found kissing a boy last night," he said, sounding repulsed at the thought of it. "He's gay."

Chapter Two

Kaitlyn stayed in her bedroom doing her homework all afternoon.

She hadn't put up any more of a fight against her mother after the morning's revelations as she'd known it would be pointless.

However, she was desperate to speak to Ellis and find out how he was coping with everything. She knew his brother's 'outing' must have been as much of a shock to him as to the rest of the town, and she couldn't imagine how he felt knowing that everyone would be gossiping about them and wanting to avoid them.

As if her thoughts had summoned him, her phone suddenly beeped on the bed beside her and she picked it up to see a message from Ellis.

I'm guessing you've heard?

Yeah. Mum and dad told me this morning. That's why she didn't let me go to yours like we planned. How are you?

He took a few moments to reply.

I'm fine. Just worried about Nicholas.

Kaitlyn hesitated before typing another message, knowing from the tone of his that he was obviously not angry with his brother. She needed to tread carefully in order to not offend him.

Is Nicholas okay?

No, he's distraught. People keep ringing our house to tell my mum we need to move. None of us can go outside in case we get lynched. It's awful. I don't know what we're gonna do now that it's out.

His wording surprised her and she quickly text back.

Did you already know?

Of course I did. We all did.

Oh. Why did you never tell me?

I wasn't sure how you'd react. Didn't want you judging him or judging me.

I would never judge you.

What about Nicholas? Has your opinion of him changed now?

Kaitlyn took too long trying to think of a suitable answer because, before she could say anything, Ellis text again.

Never mind. Your silence tells me all I need to know. Guess that's it between us then.

Her eyes widened when she read his words.

What do you mean?!

He didn't reply.

Chapter Three

Ellis and Nicholas weren't in school the following Monday, but their names were on everybody's lips.

"I heard he was doing more than just kissing that guy."

"It was a Spanish boy who's here on holiday."

"I heard there was more than just one boy involved."

"The family must have known. How could they have kept a secret like that from all of us?"

It seemed that every person Kaitlyn walked past in the corridors had something to say about what had happened, and the one thing they all agreed on was that they wanted Nicholas and his family to leave town.

Leave the country even.

Kaitlyn had never experienced a situation like it before and she had no idea what the outcome would be.

Being gay had always just been something she'd heard stories about, but they were always stories about strangers; not her best friend's brother.

She tried numerous times to text Ellis but he had ignored every single one of her messages.

Her mum had completely cut off his mum, even going so far as to block her number from the phone.

She'd asked Kaitlyn to do the same on her mobile and she'd lied and told her she had. She knew her mum wouldn't like it if she found out she was still in contact with Ellis.

She knew that associating with him or any of his family now that people knew about Nicholas would bring just as much shame on her as was already on them.

The gossiping and rumours went on for days until Kaitlyn finally went home on the Friday and found her mum and dad waiting for her in the kitchen.

"Problem solved, honey. They're moving."

She stopped in the doorway with her school blazer half way off her shoulders. "What?"

"Nicholas, Angela and Ellis. They're leaving the country."

It didn't sound real but she knew from the serious look on her mum's face that she wasn't joking.

"Are you sure? How do you know?"

"Everyone's talking about it," her dad said. "We knew they couldn't stay here for much longer. Not when Nicholas has been receiving death threats and when none of them can even show their face in public."

Kaitlyn couldn't believe it. "When are they going?"

"First thing in the morning. They've got an early flight apparently."

She looked between her parents, not understanding how they could both be so happy about their life long friends moving away, regardless of everything else that was going on.

However, she knew anything other than joy from her would just get her in trouble so she forced a smile onto her face. "Great."

Excusing herself to go and get changed out of her uniform, she quickly ran up the stairs and into her bedroom, immediately pulling out her phone to text Ellis.

You're leaving?!!!!

She didn't expect him to reply after he'd ignored her for almost a week, so she was surprised when a new notification popped up on her screen.

Yeah. Tomorrow.

It was a short and abrupt message and she knew it meant that he was still mad at her.

Weren't you at least going to say bye to me? We've been friends for thirteen years!

He took a moment to reply.

Didn't know if you'd care. Thought you'd probably want me gone as much as everyone else around here.

Of course I don't! You're my best friend! I'm going to miss you so much!

She held her breath as she waited whilst he typed again, hoping he wouldn't ask about her feelings towards Nicholas again.

Thankfully, he didn't.

I'm gonna miss you too. But we need to leave. It's not safe for us here anymore.

Tears filled her eyes, making her vision blurry as she typed her next message.

Can I see you before you go?

You sure you want to risk that?

Yes!

A few more minutes went by.

Okay. We're leaving for the airport at 7am tomorrow. Meet me in the park near my house at half 6. No one will see us there at that time. We can say a proper goodbye.

Kaitlyn felt both happy and sad at just the thought of it.

I'll be there!

Chapter Four

Kaitlyn arrived at the park early the next morning, worried that if she was even a few minutes late Ellis might assume she'd changed her mind about coming and would leave.

She still couldn't process that she was about to see her best friend for the last time. It didn't seem real.

She'd known him since she was born. He'd been two at the time and had apparently been one of the first people to hold her after her own parents.

She'd thought they would be friends forever, and it seemed unbelievably cruel that they were being torn apart by something that was neither of their faults.

As she finally spotted him strolling through the grass towards the bench where she was sat, she smiled as she took in his familiar appearance.

He was wearing a plain t-shirt and well fitted jeans, his usual style, purposely chosen so that he wouldn't stand out too much.

It was sad to think that he now stood out for all the wrong reasons.

"Hey." He smiled crookedly as he approached her before sitting beside her on the bench.

"Hi." Kaitlyn suddenly found herself fighting back the urge to cry. She didn't know how she was supposed to say goodbye to him.

"Does your mum know you're here?" he asked warily.

She shook her head, almost wanting to laugh as she imagined what her mum's reaction might have been if she'd told her she was going to meet Ellis. "No. Her and my dad are helping at the church this morning so they don't even know I'm out."

They both sat in a contemplative silence for a few moments before Ellis spoke again. "This is weird. I can't believe I'm leaving."

"I know." She turned to look at him, hoping he wouldn't notice the wetness in her eyes. "Where are you moving to?"

"America."

She raised her eyebrows in surprise. "America? Really?"

"Yeah. They're more accepting there. We won't be judged like we are here."

Kaitlyn had heard stories about how liberal America and other parts of the world were, but it had always just sounded like an intimidating place to her. A place with no rules. She couldn't imagine how horrible it would be to live somewhere like that and she felt sorry for Ellis knowing that he had to because of his brother.

"This is so unfair!" she spluttered, suddenly angry. "You and your mum shouldn't have to move away just because of Nicholas. He's seventeen, he should go on his own! This is his fault, not yours!"

Ellis frowned and she quickly stopped talking, not liking the look in his eyes.

"You think this is Nicholas's *fault*? He's gay. It's the way he was born, not something he's chosen. And it's only our fucked up country that has a problem with it! You can't blame him just because he likes guys instead of girls."

Kaitlyn stayed quiet, knowing anything else she said wouldn't be appreciated.

"I can't believe this," Ellis said, getting to his feet. "You're supposed to be my friend. You're supposed to be *Nicholas's* friend. How can you judge him like that?"

"Ellis," she started, wanting to defend herself but not being able to find the words. Eventually she just said, "It's *wrong.*"

He stared at her then as if he hated her and she shrank back against the bench, wishing she could take her words back, even if she did believe them to be true.

She didn't want to leave things with him on a bad note, but she knew she'd already spoiled their goodbye.

"I'm sorry Ellis," she said quietly.

He shook his head, obviously not wanting to hear her words. "Have a nice sheltered life Kaitlyn."

As he quickly spun around and marched away, she kept her gaze fixed on his back, willing him to look back at her one last time as silent tears started to drip down her cheeks.

His head didn't turn.

Thirteen

Years

Later

Chapter Five

2023

Kaitlyn was sitting in the living room reading one random Tuesday afternoon when the house phone began to ring on the table beside the couch, startling her for a couple of seconds until her apron clad mother rushed into the room to answer it.

"Hello?"

Her mum's smile suddenly dropped as she listened to whoever was on the line.

"Oh no. That's terrible. Let me know the details of the funeral when you have them."

At those words, Kaitlyn closed her book and sat up straight, wondering whose funeral her mum could be talking about.

The rest of the conversation didn't provide any hints so as soon as her mum hung up she asked, "Who died?"

Her mum looked at her sadly. "Ethel. She had a heart attack this morning."

Kaitlyn immediately stood up to go and hug her mum, knowing how close she and the woman had been. Ethel was Angela's mum; Ellis's grandma, so she had always had a sort of bond with Kaitlyn's family, even after the rest of her family had moved away after the scandal all those years ago.

Kaitlyn would see Ethel out and about a lot, usually either at the shops or Ethel would come into the library where she worked, and they would always have a long conversation, catching up on each other's lives.

At first Kaitlyn had wanted to speak to the woman in the hopes that she would get some news about Ellis, but after a few years it had become clear that the old woman wasn't in contact with her daughter and grandsons and she still bristled whenever any of their names were mentioned, so Kaitlyn stopped asking.

As she hugged her mum and rubbed her back in comfort, a thought suddenly came to her.

"Who was that on the phone?"

Her mum sighed. "That was Sue. Her carer. She's the one that found her."

Kaitlyn tried her best to not be disappointed. She should have known that it wouldn't have been any of Ethel's family that had called. No one had heard from them for thirteen years so she didn't know why she bothered getting her hopes up anymore.

Ellis and his family were gone.

He'd ended his friendship with Kaitlyn that day in the park when she'd watched him walk away, and the fact that he had never tried to contact her since then proved that he'd wanted nothing more to do with her.

Still, she sometimes couldn't help but wonder if he ever thought about her, just like she did with him.

She hoped so.

Just like a tiny part of her still hoped now that maybe she would see him again one day.

And that maybe his grandma's funeral would be the thing that finally brought them back together.

Chapter Six

The weather was miserable on the day of the funeral.

Thankfully the rain stopped falling before Kaitlyn and her parents left for the church, but the sky was overcast and the ground wet with puddles.

When they arrived Kaitlyn smiled as she saw the dozens of people waiting outside the church, and she couldn't help but wonder if her own funeral would be as busy some day.

Ethel had clearly touched many people's lives and it was nice to see how much she meant to the town.

The vicar was handing out a copy of the Order of Service to everyone whilst they waited for the coffin to arrive, and when Kaitlyn noticed everyone turn to look at something behind her, she guessed it was there, but when she followed the direction of the crowd's gazes she found that instead of a hearse, there were just three people standing near the church gates, dressed all in black and eyeing everyone warily.

Kaitlyn's mouth dropped open and she felt as if her blood froze as she immediately recognised them.

It was Ellis, Nicholas and Angela.

Chapter Seven

Kaitlyn couldn't trust that what she was seeing was real and she had to blink her eyes a few times to make sure that the three people wouldn't disappear.

They all looked the same in some ways; all easily identifiable by their familiar eyes and face structures; but in other ways they looked completely different.

It was Ellis that drew her attention the most and her eyes zoned in on him, examining him from head to toe.

He was taller than when she'd last seen him when he was fifteen, and his face had obviously matured, but the biggest difference to his frame was how muscular he now seemed to be. He was wearing a black suit but she could see the definition of biceps beneath the sleeves of his jacket, and firm thighs underneath his pants. The thought made her blush and she quickly looked away and focused her eyes back on his face.

His eyes were just as dark and mysterious as she remembered but the overgrown hair that fell over his forehead and landed just below his eyebrows was unfamiliar. He'd always kept his hair short and neat when he was younger, but she had to admit she liked the new look.

The thing she was most curious about was the silver hoop that was hanging from his right nostril. It seemed so out of place when compared to their surroundings, and she wondered why Angela had let him get a piercing like that when both she and Ellis must have known they weren't supposed to mark or ruin their body in any way.

The sight of the jewellery made her wonder what else might have changed about him and his beliefs over the past thirteen years, and she was intrigued to find out.

Suddenly, his eyes flashed over and caught hers, as if he'd felt her watching him, and their stares stayed locked together for a few seconds. Kaitlyn was just about to curve her lips into a friendly smile when Ellis shocked her by narrowing his gaze and turning away, dismissing her in an instant as if she meant nothing to him.

As she struggled to collect herself after the unexpected rejection, she heard her mum's sudden intake of breath as she too noticed the family standing there.

"What are they doing here?"

"Ethel was their mum and grandma," her dad reminded her.

"I don't care. Ethel didn't want anything to do with them since they left. She wouldn't have wanted them here."

Her mum started to attract people's attention around them and Kaitlyn flushed in embarrassment, avoiding meeting anyone's eyes.

"Stay away from them while they're here Kaitlyn," her mum warned her in an authoritative tone. "I don't want you mixing with people like that."

Kaitlyn nodded automatically, following her mum's orders like a little girl even though she was a twenty six year old woman.

"Don't worry mum. I won't go near them."

Chapter Eight

Ellis and his family sat on the back pew in the church. They didn't help to carry in the coffin, they didn't make any speeches, and they weren't even referred to in the vicar's eulogy.

But everyone was aware of their presence.

Kaitlyn kept seeing people sneak furtive glances towards where they sat, some just with a look of curiosity on their face and others with outright hostility.

She was careful not to turn around and look at them herself; both because her mum was sitting right beside her and because she didn't want to risk Ellis glaring at her like he had earlier, but she could *feel* him behind her.

Her body was alert in a way she'd never known it to be before, and she found herself shifting around constantly in her seat during the service, feeling self conscious about the fact that he might be watching her, but also worried that he might not have bothered to spare her a glance.

When the vicar finished talking and everyone emptied out of the church, heading towards the graveyard at the back, Kaitlyn purposely slowed her step so that she was at the back of the congregation, and she allowed her eyes to settle on her old friend and his family as they walked on the outskirts of the group.

The three of them were whispering together but seemed to be doing a good job of not letting their gazes stray from the path directly in front of them. Grief was obvious in their expressions, and she wondered what it must be like to lose someone who had completely disowned you for so many years.

As everyone gathered around the grave, Kaitlyn stood beside her mum and watched as Ethel's coffin was lowered into the ground before taking a handful of soil when it was offered to her and throwing it into the hole.

When it came to their turn, Nicholas and Angela did the same, causing people around them to mutter to themselves, but Ellis stepped back, refusing the dirt that was offered to him with a small shake of the head.

Kaitlyn watched him curiously, willing him to meet her gaze, but gave up after a few moments when it became obvious he wasn't going to.

"Let's go," her mum said once the people started to disperse. "We need to help set up for the wake."

As she followed her parents back to their car, Kaitlyn couldn't help but take one final look at Ellis and his family, hoping they too would be going to the wake; but when she saw them turn left out of the cemetery, walking in the opposite direction to where the celebration of Ethel's life was being held, she knew they must have figured out they weren't welcome there.

Chapter Nine

Kaitlyn didn't see Ellis and the others for the next couple of days, but she knew they were still in town because everywhere she went she heard people gossiping about them.

She'd found out from her mum and dad that the family had been informed of Ethel's death by her solicitor because they'd all been included in the will. They had apparently come back from New York to clear out Ethel's house and sell it to someone new, so they were planning to stay for about six weeks.

Needless to say, the town wasn't very happy about that; and there seemed to be a lot of particular outrage towards Nicholas for, in their words, 'having the cheek to come back'.

Kaitlyn was desperate to go and see her old friend but she didn't know how to go about it in a way where she wouldn't be seen and talked about herself, or where the information wouldn't get back to her mum.

She hoped Ellis might seek her out, or that she might randomly bump into him around town or in the library whilst she was at work, but she never saw him and she wondered if that was because he just didn't care about reconnecting with her, or if he just wasn't going out in public much.

She hoped for the latter.

After a few more days she began to worry that she was wasting time. She knew he wouldn't be there forever and he would soon be leaving again to go to the other side of the world, and she didn't want to miss her chance of talking to him and being able to catch up on each other's lives.

She'd never had another best friend after he'd left, and she knew she would regret it if she let him go back to America without first attempting to make things right between them.

So, one night on her way home from work, she suddenly spun around on her heel and set off in the direction of Ethel's old house where she knew Ellis, his brother and his mum were staying.

As she turned onto the street and approached the front door, she took a quick look around to check that there was no one watching and then she pressed her finger down on the bell.

Anticipation swirled in her stomach when she heard the tell tale sound of footsteps, and then the door swung open and she looked up to see the one person she'd hoped wouldn't answer.

Nicholas was standing there peering down at her with guarded eyes.

"Oh, hi Kaitlyn," he said in an accent that was a strange mix of English and American. "What are you doing here?"

She tried not to be offended about the fact that he hadn't bothered to ask how she was because she knew Ellis must have told him the things she'd said all those years ago.

"Um, I came to see you all," she said.

There was a small pause as he raised a sceptical eyebrow at her before saying, "I'll tell Ellis you're here."

He turned around and disappeared inside the house, leaving her to follow tentatively behind him as she felt her face flush from being so easily caught out.

Chapter Ten

"Ellis, you have a visitor," Kaitlyn heard Nicholas say in the distance as she stood awkwardly in the hallway, wanting to stay close to the front door in case she decided to leave at any moment.

"What? Who?" Her old friend didn't sound the same as she remembered. He too had an obvious American twang to his words, just like Nicholas.

When he appeared a moment later from a door to her left, she watched the confusion in his expression quickly turn to annoyance when he finally settled his gaze on her.

Crossing his arms, he leaned against the wall and eyed her as if she was his enemy, instead of his childhood friend. "What do you want Kaitlyn?"

Her embarrassment was immediate, and she wished she'd never decided to visit. "Um, I don't know," she muttered nervously. "I just wanted to see you. I wanted to talk."

He raised his eyebrows patronisingly. "What about? We don't have anything in common anymore."

It was her turn to frown. "You don't know that. We might."

His only response was to scoff.

They stood not speaking and avoiding looking at each other for a minute or so, but then the tension was finally broken when Angela walked out of the kitchen with a broad smile on her face.

"Kaitlyn." She rushed over to sweep her up into a hug which Kaitlyn automatically returned, feeling almost as if no time had passed since she'd received the same sort of hugs when she was thirteen. Angela pulled back and grasped hold of her upper arms, looking her up and down. "Oh you look so grown up! You're so pretty! I'm so glad you came, honey. I was desperate to speak to you when I saw you at mum's funeral but I knew it was probably best if I didn't."

Kaitlyn gave her a sad, understanding smile. "I'm sorry about Ethel," she said, choosing to not address the other problem just yet.

"Thank you dear." Angela sighed. "I know I hadn't spoken to my mum for over ten years but it still feels weird to know we're not even sharing the same world anymore. As soon as I heard from the solicitor I knew we'd have to come back here, no matter how much trouble it might cause."

"Are you talking about me?" Nicholas suddenly said, coming back into view with a smirk on his face.

Kaitlyn was surprised he could joke about himself like that, and when she saw the same kind of amusement on Ellis's and Angela's faces she felt like the odd one out.

"It's okay Kaitlyn," Angela said in a calm voice, drawing her focus back to the other woman. "You know it's just Nicholas, right? He's still the same boy you grew up with. Nothing about him has really changed."

Kaitlyn felt her face grow hot as the three of them stared at her whilst she struggled to think of something to say.

She knew that what Angela had said was true, but it was difficult for her to see things in the same way as them when she had been taught her whole life that being gay was wrong.

As her gaze found Nicholas's once more, she did her best to forget about what she knew of his sexuality, and she just saw him as the boy she'd used to play hide and seek with. The boy who had protected her from bullies in school and who had helped clean scrapes on her knees when she'd fallen over.

The boy who'd been her friend.

And then suddenly, as she stared into his kind eyes, an overwhelming wave of regret washed over her, and she burst into uncontrollable tears before running into his arms.

Chapter Eleven

"I'm so sorry," Kaitlyn sobbed as she squeezed Nicholas tightly. "I'm sorry for everything I said about you back then. I was young and stupid and I blamed you for making Ellis move away. I wasn't thinking clearly. I was in shock and my mum was telling me to stay away from you..." She broke off as another flood of tears started pouring from her eyes.

"Ssh," Nicholas soothed, rubbing her back once he'd got over the initial surprise of having her grab him like that. "It's okay. I understand. It's not your fault."

When she'd finally managed to compose herself, she pulled back and saw Nicholas and his mum watching her with concern.

As she looked across at Ellis, she couldn't read his expression and she wondered what he was thinking about her sudden meltdown.

"I missed you all so much," she told them all as she looked between them. "I'm sorry we never kept in contact."

"We missed you too honey." Angela came forward to hug her again. "And you don't have to apologise. Your mum wouldn't have let you keep in contact even if you'd wanted to."

Kaitlyn knew she was right.

"Do you want a drink, love?" Angela asked, leading her into the living room and gesturing for her to take a seat on the couch. "Or do you need to go home?"

Kaitlyn knew that the longer she stayed out, the more she'd risk her mum finding out about her visit, but she wasn't ready to leave just yet and she felt stupid having to admit to the clearly liberal family in front of her that she still had a curfew.

"Um, can I just have some water?"

Angela smiled. "Of course."

When she was left alone in the room with Ellis and Nicholas, she looked between both boys awkwardly, wanting to ask so many questions but not knowing where to start.

She also couldn't figure out if Ellis had forgiven her like the other two so she wasn't sure how to act around him and she didn't want to make a fool of herself by trying to talk like they used to only to have him reject her.

"So, Kaitlyn," Nicholas started, taking a seat beside her. "What are you up to these days?"

"Err, well, I work in the library three days a week, and, um, I still read a lot and like going for walks."

"Oh. Cool." The way he said it made it sound like he thought her life was anything but. "Do you still live at home? Or are you married now?"

At that she let out an embarrassed giggle. "No, I'm not married. My mum's still as protective as ever, but she's agreed that once I get to thirty she and my dad will find me a husband."

She flashed her eyes up to Ellis when she heard him make a scoffing noise and as she looked between the brothers, seeing the obvious pity in their expressions, she suddenly felt her face heat with humiliation.

"What's wrong with that?" she asked quietly, starting to doubt herself.

Nicholas quickly shook his head, looking as though he was about to reassure her, but Ellis cut in before he could.

"It's so *stupid*," he spat as he stared at her nastily. "Do you realise how pathetic that all sounds? You're twenty six years old for crying out loud!"

"Ellis!" Angela suddenly shouted as she reappeared from the kitchen, holding Kaitlyn's glass of water. "Leave her alone. It's not her fault. She's never known anything different."

"I'm trying to give her a reality check," he protested. "She needs to realise how weird it is to be doing nothing with her life other than waiting around for her mum and dad to find her a husband."

"It's none of our business," Angela said sternly. "That's the way things are here, and you would have grown up thinking the same way if we had never moved away."

Kaitlyn hated how they were discussing her as if she wasn't there, and she couldn't bear to hear any more of what was being said about the life she led, which she'd never thought to question before that moment.

"Um, I'm gonna go." She stood up quickly and started moving towards the door."

"No, Kaitlyn, wait." Angela followed after her but both boys stayed in the living room. "Please don't go yet."

"I have to. It's getting late and my mum will be expecting me home." She tried to say the words as quietly as possible so Ellis might not hear.

Angela looked disappointed. "Okay. But why don't you come round for dinner tomorrow? I'll cook us all something nice and we can have a proper catch up."

Kaitlyn hesitated. She loved the sound of the plan but she wasn't sure what she'd tell her mum as an excuse for where she was. And on top of that, she didn't particularly like the idea of being subjected to more of Ellis's insults.

"I'll see if I'm free," she said finally, hoping Angela wouldn't question her more and make her admit that she was *always* free.

"Great. Well, if you can make it, come round for about six 'o' clock." Angela smiled and opened the front door for her, not acknowledging Kaitlyn's furtive look around the street to check that no one was watching as she stepped outside.

"Bye then," Kaitlyn said awkwardly. "I'll see you soon."

As she walked away she hoped her words were true.

She was desperate to spend as much time with the family as possible before they had to leave again and so she decided in that moment that she would tell whatever lies she had to in order to go round for dinner the next night.

Ellis's scornful face came to the forefront of her mind, making her stomach twist with an unfamiliar emotion. She hated that he had treated her so cruelly and she wanted to fix his opinion of her, but she wasn't sure how to.

She'd heard stories over the years about how 'backwards' England apparently was compared to the rest of the world, but as she had never left the country, she had nothing to compare it to and therefore didn't understand what was so different and apparently pathetic about her lifestyle.

But she was determined to find out.

And then maybe she would get her best friend back.

Chapter Twelve

Kaitlyn wasn't in work the next day so she had a small lie in and then went for a walk around lunchtime.

She'd spent the whole of the night before trying to think of a lie to tell her mum and dad for where she would be going that night, but when she'd seen the calendar in the kitchen that morning she'd grinned widely when she'd realised that her parents had plans to go their friend's house for the night, meaning that they would probably be out until late and therefore would never even realise that Kaitlyn had left the house.

As she walked along the familiar streets of the town, she smiled to herself at the prospect of seeing her old friends again and started to plan what she could wear.

Although she'd never been the sort of person to care much about her appearance before, she suddenly felt the need to dress nice because she wanted to impress Ellis.

She didn't really understand why his opinion mattered to her so much, but there was something about his dark eyes and intense gaze that sent a sort of thrill through her and made her want to show him that she wasn't really as boring as he thought she was.

Spotting a nearby clothes shop, she paused outside the window and looked in at all the elegant dresses which seemed so much more interesting than the usual jeans and t-shirt that she wore most days.

Deciding on the spur of the moment to treat herself, she wrapped her fingers around the door handle and went inside.

Kaitlyn arrived at Ethel's old house at only a couple of minutes after 6pm and she quietly knocked on the door, hoping to not draw any attention to herself from the other people who lived on the street.

Angela greeted her with a warm smile and pulled her into another hug as she shut the door behind them.

"You came! I'm so glad." She ran her eyes up and down Kaitlyn's body. "You look lovely in that dress. I hope you didn't feel like you had to dress up just to come and see us, though."

Kaitlyn gave her a nervous smile but didn't respond as Angela began to call up the stairs to her sons, letting them know she was there.

Nicholas came bounding down a moment later with a broad grin on his face which Kaitlyn automatically returned, trying to ignore the voice in her mind which was still trying to make her feel awkward around him.

They all went to sit in the living room and Angela told her that she was making a chicken roast before she went out to the hallway again.

"Ellis! Come down!"

Kaitlyn tried to not show her embarrassment about the fact that he obviously didn't care about seeing her, but she couldn't help but wonder why he was so disinterested in her when it was the two of them who shared the most history out of everyone in the house.

Finally, a couple of minutes later, they heard his footsteps practically stomping down the stairs and he appeared in the room, immediately locking eyes with Kaitlyn.

She gave him a tentative smile but then her attention was quickly drawn down his body, past the glinting hoop in his nose, to his arms which she was able to see properly for the first time since they'd come back because he was wearing a short sleeved t-shirt.

Her eyes widened in both surprise and intrigue as she examined the two large drawings he had on his body, one on the inside of either forearm. They didn't look to be of anything in particular, just a mixture of shapes and patterns, but they were big and bold and almost intimidating.

She'd never seen anything like it before and she wondered why he'd marked himself in that way.

Was it supposed to be some kind of statement or protest against his old life, just like the ring in his nostril?

"What are those?" she asked, unable to take her stare off them as she tried to take in every detail.

Ellis let out a small chuckle. "They're tattoos."

She'd heard the word before and understood them to be some sort of brand that people put on themselves.

"So, they're permanent? You can't wash them off?"

She met his eyes again, seeing the amusement in his expression as he shook his head.

"Who put them on you?"

"My mate did one, and I did the other," he said, surprising her. "It's what I do for work. I'm a tattoo artist."

It was almost as if he was speaking a foreign language.

"Do you have any more?"

"One on my back." He shrugged like it was no big deal. "I might get a few more eventually."

She turned to Angela and Nicholas. "Do you have them too?"

They all laughed.

"Mum doesn't," Nicholas said before he pulled up the bottom of his jeans, revealing a large tattoo on his outer calf. "I just have this one so far."

Kaitlyn couldn't help but reach out and start tracing the pattern with her fingers, marvelling at how the skin felt normal, before she quickly pulled away in embarrassment. "Sorry."

Nicholas laughed again. "It's alright. They must seem weird if you've never seen them before."

Kaitlyn smiled but didn't say anything more on the matter, knowing she'd probably already made herself look stupid enough.

"Well," Angela said after a moment, changing the subject. "Why don't the three of you sit down and start to have a catch up and I'll go and finish cooking."

"Do you want help?" Kaitlyn asked automatically, knowing women were usually expected to be in the kitchen and the men were the ones who were supposed to sit down chatting.

But Karen just waved her away. "It's fine, honey. I can do it." She gave her a conspiratorial wink. "We do a lot of things differently nowadays. You'll see."

Chapter Thirteen

"So, tell me about New York," Kaitlyn said eagerly. "What's it like to live there?"

"It's amazing." Nicholas smiled fondly as he talked about it and she couldn't help but feel jealous, unable to imagine herself acting the same way if someone foreign asked her to describe England. "It's so different to here. Everyone's so laid back, and there's always something going on there. You could never get bored."

"You should visit one day," Ellis suggested, but as she looked across at him she couldn't tell if he was being serious or if he was teasing her, knowing the chances of that ever happening were almost impossible.

Did he just want her to admit that her mum wouldn't let her?

She wasn't sure, but she didn't say the words aloud just in case.

Turning back to Nicholas, she asked another question. "What do you do for work there?"

"I own a music shop," he told her proudly.

"Really?" It sounded so exciting. "By yourself?"

"No, with my boyfriend."

Kaitlyn felt her face fall at that word but she quickly recovered herself and was grateful that Nicholas didn't acknowledge it. "Oh, so, you're courting?"

He laughed for a reason that she didn't understand. "Yeah. But in America they just call it dating."

Filing that fact away, she turned to Ellis. "What about you? Are you...dating?"

His lips twitched in amusement but he shook his head. "Not at the moment."

Kaitlyn felt a sort of relief at hearing he was unattached, although she didn't understand why.

She also didn't like the way he'd said 'not at the moment', meaning that he had 'dated' in the past.

She wondered what kind of woman he found attractive, but then told herself it shouldn't matter to her and quickly rid the thought from her mind.

"Dinner's ready," Angela suddenly announced from somewhere not too far away, breaking the silence that had fallen between the three old friends.

Kaitlyn followed both boys into the dining room where they found four steaming plates of food laid out for them.

Just like they'd done when they were all younger, Angela and Nicholas immediately sat down next to each other, leaving her to sit beside Ellis, but unlike in the past, she felt an immediate tension coming off of his body as she accidentally brushed her arm against his whilst she arranged herself in her seat.

"Sorry," she said stupidly, quickly avoiding eye contact and concentrating on her food.

Ellis was mostly silent during the meal, and Kaitlyn spent her time listening to Nicholas's and Angela's stories about America, fascinated by the knowledge that women could drive over there and that they had important roles in society.

As she digested each new bit of information she couldn't help but wonder if Ellis had been right.

If maybe her life in England *was* boring.

If maybe she'd been sheltered from the outside world for all the wrong reasons.

Chapter Fourteen

"That was lovely," Kaitlyn said as Angela cleared her plate away. "Thank you so much."

The older woman smiled. "No problem at all. It's nice having you here."

As Kaitlyn glanced at the clock, her stomach sank at the realisation that it was time for her to go home.

She didn't want to risk her mum and dad getting back before she did.

"I should go before it gets too dark," she said, making her excuses as she stood up from the table.

"Oh, it's a shame we don't have our cars here," Angela said, pulling a face. "One of us could have driven you home otherwise."

"I'll walk you," Ellis suddenly announced, surprising Kaitlyn.

"Oh. Right. Okay," she stuttered as he went to get his coat from the hallway.

She hugged Angela and Nicholas goodbye, promising to see them soon, before going to join Ellis as he opened the door and stepped outside.

Once he'd closed the door behind them, Kaitlyn immediately noticed the atmosphere between them grow heavier.

Ellis had walked her home dozens of times when they were both younger, but things weren't as comfortable as they were back then and so it felt like a completely different situation.

"Do you remember how to get to my house?" she asked, making conversation in order to ease the awkwardness.

He nodded. "I remember everything about this town."

She got the feeling he was talking about more than just knowing his way around, and her curiosity got piqued.

"Why do you talk as if you hate this place so much?"

He let out an almost cynical laugh. "Why do you think? The town basically forced us out of the country."

She could understand that but it seemed like there was more to it. "Is that the only reason?"

He sighed and looked at her out of the corner of his eye. "No. It's the whole country that I hate." He came to a sudden halt and stared at her intensely as he spoke his next words.

"You have no idea what's really out there Kaitlyn. What life could really be like for you. You don't realise it because you've never been anywhere other than England, but you're being held back here. You're being *oppressed*."

She almost flinched at the word. "No, I'm not." She hated how defensive she sounded. "People who are oppressed have miserable, lonely lives."

He raised an eyebrow at her. "Are you honestly saying you don't?"

Kaitlyn quickly looked away, avoiding his knowing expression. "I'm happy here," she told him. "And so is everyone else who lives here."

Ellis stayed silent, clearly not believing her, and it made her inexplicably angry.

"Anyway, who says England is living the wrong way and everyone else in the world is right? Maybe it's the opposite. Maybe America and other countries should follow our rules."

"They did a couple of hundred years ago," Ellis reminded her. "But they've moved with the times. England hasn't."

She didn't want to hear any more, and she'd run out of ways to defend her country, so she marched off, leaving him to follow.

"England isn't that bad," she muttered, almost to herself. "Are you really saying you missed nothing about your home country?"

"No."

The lack of hesitation before his answer made her come to a standstill once more and she gazed up at him, hoping to not show how hurt she was by his words.

"Did you not even miss *me*?"

His expression turned serious in an instant and she watched his pupils dilate as he stared into her eyes with a look she'd never seen before.

"*Of course* I missed you," he told her earnestly. "More than you could ever understand."

Kaitlyn was taken aback by the sudden passion in his voice as he said the words and she opened her mouth, trying to think of a way to respond, but was quickly cut off when Ellis took an unexpected step closer and pressed his lips softly against hers.

Chapter Fifteen

The kiss lasted for only a fraction of a second before Kaitlyn ripped her mouth away.

"What on earth are you doing?"

She expected Ellis to look contrite and to apologise but instead his eyes darkened and he took another step forwards, causing her to become trapped against him and the wall behind her.

"Please Kaitlyn," he whispered in a voice she barely recognised. "Let me. You'll like it, I promise."

She wasn't sure why his words persuaded her, but when he leaned in again and placed his mouth back on hers she found herself closing her eyes and letting her body relax against his, not putting up a protest this time.

Ellis brought his hand up to gently cup her cheek as his mouth began to move over hers, and she tilted her head towards his touch, enjoying the feel of his skin on her cheek and the tiny sparks she could feel in her lips each time they brushed against his.

Almost on instinct, she let her mouth fall open further and began to slowly follow his movements, causing him to make a strange noise in the back of his throat which sent an unfamiliar sensation through her body.

Just as she found herself giving into the urge to wrap her arms around his neck in order to pull him closer, Ellis suddenly plunged his tongue into her mouth, shocking her and making her jump back with a gasp.

"Stop it!" she told him. "You shouldn't be touching me like that."

He narrowed his eyes. "Why not?"

"Because," she said, feeling flustered. "It's wrong. We're not married or even engaged. And we're in the street where anyone could see."

He didn't seem at all bothered by what she was saying and instead just crossed his arms in an almost challenging way. "Are you telling me you didn't like it?"

Kaitlyn swallowed nervously. Choosing to avoid giving a proper answer she just said, "You're my friend, Ellis. Why would you do something like that?"

He laughed scornfully and shook his head. "We're not friends, Kaitlyn. We haven't been for thirteen years; and even back then I wanted more from you. I just didn't understand it until I left."

His words confused her and made her head spin as she tried to make sense of them whilst still trying to process the kiss that had just happened.

"I need to go home Ellis," she said, knowing that she wouldn't be able to think properly until she was away from his intense stare.

His expression went blank. "Fine. Go. Make sure your mummy and daddy don't find out where you've been."

She frowned at his patronising tone, even though she knew he was right.

Without bothering to say goodbye, she turned and walked away, purposely going as slow as possible so that he wouldn't think she was in a rush.

But as soon as she'd rounded a corner and was out of his line of sight, she abruptly started sprinting and didn't stop until she was safe inside her empty house.

Chapter Sixteen

Kaitlyn spent most of the night tossing and turning in bed, replaying the incident with Ellis over and over again in her mind.

She didn't know what to think about his actions and the things he'd said to her, but one thing she did know was that it had been wrong for him to kiss her.

And it had been even *more* wrong for her to kiss him back, even if she didn't do it for longer than a few seconds.

Her heart wanted to memorise every detail about what it had felt like to have his mouth on hers, but her brain knew she needed to forget and pretend that it had never happened.

If her mum found out she'd been doing something like that, she'd probably forbid her from ever leaving the house alone again; and if the people in the town knew about it they would shun her in the same way they'd shunned Nicholas and his family all those years ago.

After all, no one wanted to be associated with a whore who went around kissing boys she wasn't betrothed to.

When she got out of bed the next morning after only managing to get a couple of hours of sleep, Kaitlyn promised herself that she would never think about the kiss again, and that she would do her best to avoid Ellis and the others for the rest of the time they were in town.

But that was easier said than done when, to her surprise, the family turned up at church that morning.

It was her mum who first drew her attention to them.

"I don't believe it," she'd said from her position beside Kaitlyn in the middle pew. "How dare they come here."

Kaitlyn had followed her glare to find the two boys and their mum entering the church and taking a seat on the back row.

She was just as shocked as her mum to see them there.

The last place she would have expected to accidentally bump into Ellis was in *church*.

As if she'd spoken aloud, his head suddenly turned and his eyes latched onto hers, keeping her trapped in his intense stare for a few seconds until she finally forced herself to look away.

She quickly checked that her mum and dad hadn't seen the moment, but thankfully they were too busy chatting to others in the congregation, discussing the possibility of having the vicar ask the family to leave.

Luckily, that didn't happen, but everyone made sure to give Ellis, Nicholas and Angela as many dirty looks as possible throughout the service in order to make it clear to them that they weren't welcome there.

Everyone except Kaitlyn, that is.

She didn't turn around once and was careful to keep her gaze trained on the vicar, even though she could *feel* Ellis's eyes on her, willing her to look at him.

She was aware of his presence in a way she'd never been with another person before, and she wondered how one small kiss could have the power to send her emotions into such a frenzy, and could affect her perception of him so much.

Before, he'd always been her childhood friend. The boy who she'd fallen out with, but who she'd looked back on with fond memories.

So why had one forbidden kiss made him feel like so much more than just a friend to her?

Why did she suddenly *want him* to be much more than that?

Chapter Seventeen

When the service ended Kaitlyn realised that she hadn't listened to a word of it because she'd been so distracted by the idea of Ellis watching her.

Her mum was still shooting hateful looks towards the back of the church as they all stood up to leave.

"They've got a cheek coming in a sacred place like this," she said venomously. "That boy definitely doesn't belong in a place like this. How dare he claim to still be a christian when we know what he does in private."

The urge to defend Nicholas rose up inside Kaitlyn but then quickly diminished when she realised it would be a pointless exercise and would likely only end up getting her in trouble with her parents.

Instead, she stayed silent and continued to listen to the spiteful words that everyone around her was saying as they all huddled together to discuss the 'issue'.

"I think we should go and talk to the vicar now," one man suggested. "It was too late for him to do anything about it when they were already here, but I bet he can stop them from coming again."

The group all seemed to think that was a good idea and so they marched off to the front of the church, surrounded the vicar and all started to speak at once while they gesticulated wildly.

Kaitlyn remained where she was, not knowing if her mum had expected her to follow, but also not wanting to get involved.

She took a quick glance back over her shoulder to see that Ellis, his brother and mum had left so she decided that it would be safe for her to do the same.

However, she only made it a short way down the road before a tall figure fell into step beside her.

She purposely didn't look in his direction and just continued to walk forwards, heading towards her house which was only a couple of streets away.

"What do you want, Ellis?"

She almost told him that he shouldn't be speaking to her in public but she didn't want to sound rude or like she was as judgmental as everyone else in the town.

"I just wanted to talk to you," he said. She could sense him trying to catch her eye but refused to turn her head. "I didn't think you'd appreciate me coming up to you in church when your mum was there."

She couldn't help but laugh as she imagined the look of horror that would have been on her mum's face if he had done that. "Yeah, that was probably a smart idea." She didn't give him a chance to say anything else because she quickly added, "What were you three even doing at church?"

"We're still christians," he told her. "We still have a right to go to church as much as anyone else does. The fact that Nicholas is gay doesn't change that."

"Yeah, but." she broke off, knowing she had no argument other than explaining other people's prejudice against them going.

"Anyway, that's not what I wanted to talk to you about," he said, steering back to the original conversation which she'd tried to avoid.

He wrapped his fingers around her upper arm to try to get her to stop walking but she jerked away from him as if he'd burned her. "What are you doing? You can't just grab hold of me in the street like that."

He held up his hands in a placating gesture. "I'm sorry. I wasn't grabbing hold of you. I just wanted you to look at me."

But the problem was that she didn't want to look at him, because then she might have to admit to herself just how attractive she suddenly found him; and then she would have to worry about how wrong it was for her to think like that.

"You need to leave me alone, Ellis," she told him, unable to meet his eyes. "What you did last night was wrong. If someone had seen it or if they saw us together right now, it would ruin my reputation. You might not care what people think about you anymore because you no longer live here, but I do, and I can't have people thinking badly of me like that."

His disgusted expression told her exactly how stupid he thought she was being, but she paid it no attention and just set off walking again, hoping he wouldn't follow.

Unfortunately, she wasn't that lucky.

"Kaitlyn!" he shouted, almost as if he was trying to be as loud as possible so that people would hear. "Stop!"

She was forced to do what he wanted so that he would quiet down.

"Shut up," she said angrily as she stomped back towards him. "I've told you I don't want to talk to you."

"No, you've told me the reasons you *shouldn't* talk to me. But you never actually said you didn't *want* me to. Just like you never actually said you didn't enjoy that kiss last night."

Kaitlyn felt herself flush at his words, both in embarrassment and because she didn't understand how he could be so casual when discussing something so intimate.

She knew he was right with everything he'd said, but she didn't see the point in admitting it because either way it wouldn't change anything between them.

She let out a heavy sigh, suddenly feeling exhausted and desperate for him to stop talking and listen to her.

"*Please* Ellis," she said, imploring him with her eyes. "Please just let me forget about it, okay? Just let me pretend that it never happened."

He stayed silent for a few more moments, watching her carefully as his probing gaze examined every inch of her expression.

"Fine," he said eventually. "It never happened."

She gave him a grateful smile and was just about to say thank you when a screeching voice suddenly sounded behind them.

"Kaitlyn! What are you doing? Get away from him!"

She turned in horror to see her mum and dad storming towards them with a look of thunder on their faces.

Chapter Eighteen

"Fuck," Kaitlyn heard Ellis say as they watched her parents approaching.

Her mum reached them first and quickly stood in front of Kaitlyn, squaring up to Ellis as if she wasn't at all intimidated by how much larger he was than her.

"Why are you talking to my daughter?" she asked him, practically spitting the words.

"I just wanted to say hi," Ellis said, managing to sound genuine.

But her mum didn't believe a word of it.

"Was he harassing you?" she asked her daughter.

"No!" Kaitlyn exclaimed. "We just walked past each other so he stopped to say hello."

Her mum's eyes narrowed. "Are you sure that's all it was?"

Kaitlyn nodded.

"Well, you should have ignored him," her mum said, still angry. "I've told you not to talk to him."

"It was my fault," Ellis quickly said before Kaitlyn could try to defend herself. "I blocked her path so that she'd be forced to acknowledge me. She tried to ignore me but I wouldn't let her."

Her mum easily believed that story.

"Stay away from her," she said threateningly. "If I find out you've tried to speak to her again, I'll call the police and get a restraining order against you."

Kaitlyn wasn't sure that such a thing would be possible but she didn't want to point that out when her mother was already in a bad mood.

"I won't," Ellis promised, sounding so believable that Kaitlyn's stomach suddenly sank at the thought of not getting to see him again before he left.

"Good. Let's go Kaitlyn." her mum grabbed her arm and led her away like a child in trouble, whilst her dad followed obediently behind them.

Chapter Nineteen

"I was hoping I'd find you here."

Kaitlyn turned away from the shelves she was stacking books on to find Angela standing at the end of the aisle with the usual friendly smile on her face.

"Oh, um, hi."

She felt uncomfortable about being sought out in her place of work and she quickly took a look around to make sure that no one was watching.

"Don't worry," Angela said with a wave of her hand. "If anyone asks, you can just say I asked for your help finding a book."

Kaitlyn smiled at the older woman, grateful that she understood her predicament.

"Did you want help finding a book?"

"No. I just haven't seen you for a few days so I wanted to invite you round to have dinner with us tonight. It's my birthday."

"Oh."

Kaitlyn's automatic response was to agree to the plan because she didn't like the idea of letting someone down on their birthday, but she couldn't help but worry about her mum potentially finding out about it and following through on her threat to Ellis.

"I don't know. My mum.." she started to explain but Angela just shook her head.

"Don't worry about her. Ellis told me what she said to him the other day but there's nothing she could get the police to do, I promise."

Kaitlyn knew that Angela was probably right, but she also knew how tenacious her mum could be when it came to getting something she wanted.

"Okay," she agreed reluctantly, still unsure about whether she actually wanted to go because it would mean dealing with Ellis. "I'll be there. What time?"

After agreeing for her to go round straight after work, Angela discreetly disappeared, slipping out from between the rows of bookshelves and leaving the library before most people probably realised she had even been there.

Kaitlyn puzzled over what to tell her parents for the rest of the day.

She couldn't tell them she was working late because they knew what time the library closed.

She couldn't tell them she was going out with a friend because they knew she didn't have any.

So what could she possibly say?

By the end of the day she still hadn't decided but she got her phone out of her pocket as she left the library, knowing she would have to make something up on the spot.

However, she never got the chance and instead quickly put her mobile away when she found her dad standing outside waiting for her.

"Dad, what are you doing here?"

He held up a bag of shopping. "You're mum sent me out to get stuff for dinner so I thought I'd come and meet you while I was nearby."

"Oh. Great."

He had done the same thing only a handful of times before, but it was just her luck that he would choose that day to do it again.

As they walked home in a comfortable silence, her mind spun as she tried to think of different excuses she could make to get away.

But nothing came to her.

Resigning herself to having to stay in with her family for the evening, she took the bag of shopping from her dad. "I'll carry this."

They ate early like they'd always done since she was a kid, so it was only 6pm by the time the table had been cleared and her mum was washing up in the kitchen.

"I'm not feeling very well," she told her parents. "I think I'm gonna go and lie down for a while. Maybe have an early night."

Her mum smiled. "Good idea."

Kaitlyn wasn't feeling ill at all but she just didn't want to spend the rest of her night watching rubbish television with her mum and dad and so she sloped off up the stairs to her bedroom.

As she lay back on her pillows, she stared at her phone, wishing she had a way to contact Angela, Nicholas or Ellis to explain why she hadn't gone to their house as planned.

She hated the idea of seeming rude and of them thinking she had just decided not to spend time with them.

And she resented the fact that she had no real freedom in her life. At least not like the freedom she'd heard of in the stories about the world outside England.

Suddenly feeling the need to be rebellious for once, she quickly sat up and walked over to her bedroom window, looking down at the ground below to figure out if she would be able to climb down without risking serious injury.

She didn't recognise herself at that moment, and she knew she would probably regret her actions later, but her mind was set on following through with her plan, regardless of the consequences.

So, with one final look over her shoulder to check that her mum or dad weren't about to burst in her room and catch her, she quickly lifted her leg and lowered it over the window frame.

Chapter Twenty

Kaitlyn felt an unbelievable sense of exhilaration as she ran through the outskirts of town, being careful to not be seen by anyone who might know her or her parents.

She had never snuck out of the house before or broken any of her mum's rules, so she had never known how liberating it would feel to do so.

She didn't allow herself to worry about her mum going up to her bedroom and finding her missing, or about how she was going to sneak back in the house later.

All she cared about was that she'd taken control of her own life for once.

She was going to see her friends, no matter how much trouble she might get in because of it.

By the time she reached the house she was out of breath and had a stitch so she took a moment to try and recover before finally knocking on the door.

Ellis answered and frowned when he saw her. "We thought you weren't coming."

Without waiting for an invitation, she pushed past him into the house, seeing Nicholas and Angela coming out of the kitchen looking just as confused as Ellis.

"I'm sorry I'm late," she told them, still panting slightly. "My dad met me after work and walked me home so I had to eat with them. But I managed to sneak out afterwards."

"You snuck out?" Ellis asked, looking almost impressed.

She nodded. "I climbed out of my bedroom window."

They all looked amused by that part of the story and she couldn't help but feel quite proud of herself.

"Have you already eaten?" she asked Angela.

"No. We were just about to order something. Are you still hungry?"

"After running the whole way here, I am," Kaitlyn said, causing them to laugh.

She followed them into the kitchen to look at the menu for the burger place they were ordering from.

"Have you eaten from here before?" Nicholas asked her.

"No. My mum doesn't let us have takeaways."

He rolled his eyes playfully and she smiled.

After Angela had placed the order, she hung up the phone and announced. "They said it will be about half an hour."

Wondering what they'd be doing in the meantime, Kaitlyn stood awkwardly for a moment before Ellis suddenly suggested, "Do you want to come and hang out in my room?"

She stared at him, open-mouthed, waiting for his mum to shout at him, but Angela just looked at her expectantly.

"What? No! Of course not," Kaitlyn said, stumbling over her words. "I can't be in your bedroom *alone* with you."

Surprisingly, no one else in the room seemed to agree with her.

"It's fine, honey," Angela reassured her. "We don't follow all those silly old traditions anymore. It's another thing that's only still done in England."

Kaitlyn couldn't believe it and she stood staring between the three of them for a moment as she tried to decide what to do.

On the one hand, she knew it wouldn't feel right to go up to Ellis's room with him; especially when it would only be the two of them. She'd been taught that any girl who acted like that would be considered a whore and that it would be assumed she was getting up to bad stuff with the boy.

But on the other hand, she was curious to see what Ellis's bedroom looked like and to see more of his possessions so she could find out more about the man he was today.

"Alright," she agreed quietly, still not entirely comfortable with the idea but not wanting to look strange in front of them when they obviously believed it was a completely normal thing to do.

Ellis looked at her warmly and then led the way out of the room and up the stairs until they were standing outside his bedroom door.

"Ladies first," he told her, gesturing for her to go inside.

Her whole body tingled as she wrapped her fingers around the handle and pushed into the room, feeling him enter behind her as the door closed softly, separating them from the others in the house.

She knew that, regardless of what Angela had said, being alone with him like that was forbidden; at least in *her* country.

But that somehow made it all the more exciting.

Chapter Twenty One

"Nice room," Kaitlyn commented, as a way to fill the silence.

Ellis laughed. "No it's not. You can tell it's a grandma's house."

She had to agree with him about that.

Everything in the room seemed to be floral other than the few obvious things that belonged to him.

"Sorry, she said awkwardly, feeling her cheeks heat. "I'm just nervous."

She regretted the words as soon as they came out of her mouth.

Ellis slowly moved to stand in front of her, waiting for her to meet his gaze before he asked, "Why are you nervous?"

"I don't know." She shrugged. "It's just weird being in here with you. I've never done anything like this before."

He tilted his head as his eyes probed into her. "Are you worried I'm gonna kiss you again?"

Kaitlyn looked away and cleared her throat. "You promised we could forget about that."

Ellis sighed heavily. "You're right. Sorry."

He quickly crossed the room to put the television on before sitting down on the edge of the bed and patting the space beside him in an apparent invitation.

Kaitlyn slowly went over to join him, purposely putting as much distance as possible between their bodies as she sat down.

She stayed quiet as Ellis began to flick through the channels, but couldn't help but notice the irritation on his face as he seemed to struggle to find something to watch.

"The TV over here is shit," he moaned. "Everything is censored."

The word piqued her curiosity. "What do you mean?"

He turned to her, looking panicked for a moment as if he thought he might have said too much. "Um, well, they purposely edit shows over here so that nothing inappropriate is shown."

"Inappropriate? Like what?"

She was surprised when she saw his cheeks turn red with embarrassment. "Like things that might show a different way of life to what you have over here. And, you know, *rude* stuff."

"Like people swearing?"

He let out a laugh and ran a hand through his dark hair. "No, just like kissing scenes and stuff like that."

"Oh." It was her turn to be embarrassed. "So, in America they show stuff like that on television?"

He nodded. "Believe me, they show a lot more than that sometimes."

She couldn't imagine it.

She knew that married couples kissed behind closed doors, and she knew that there was something a man and woman had to do in order to make a baby, although she wasn't sure what; but it was hard to believe that such intimate things would ever be shown on television.

Especially between two strangers.

Ellis watched her as she processed what she'd been told. "What are you thinking?"

Kaitlyn shrugged. "I'm not sure. I don't really know what to think." Suddenly having an idea, she asked, "Do you have anything on your laptop you can show me like that?"

He frowned. "Err, no. While I'm here I can only connect to the internet in England so that's all censored too."

"But do you not have videos saved on there?" She stood up and went to collect the laptop from his bedside table.

Ellis quickly followed her. "Not those kinds of videos," he said, trying to pull it from her arms.

Something about the panic on his face made her curious and she refused to let go. "What are you hiding on here?"

"Nothing."

She didn't believe him. "Come on, tell me. Please. I thought you wanted me to learn about what the outside world is like?"

He laughed awkwardly. "Yeah, but I didn't mean you should see stuff like *that*."

"Stuff like what?"

When it became obvious he wasn't going to answer she quickly ripped the laptop from his hold and ran to the other side of the bed, opening the screen and clicking on his videos folder before he managed to reach her and grab the device back.

But she'd seen enough.

"What are those?" She asked, shocked by the small thumbnails she'd just seen. "Why do you have videos of naked people on there?"

Ellis looked mortified. "It doesn't matter. It's just gonna freak you out so will you just forget about it?"

She stood her ground. "No, I want to see them."

She wasn't sure why she was so curious about them, but the forbidden nature of the videos mixed with Ellis's strange reaction made her desperate to find out more.

He didn't respond to her request, but also didn't put up a fight when she reached to take the laptop from him once more before sitting down on the bed and re-opening the folder she'd found.

She double clicked on the first video and stared in a horrified fascination as a naked man and woman popped up on the screen, moving together in a way she didn't understand and making strange noises that evoked an unfamiliar sensation within her body.

"What are they doing?" she asked, unable to look away from the video even though part of her was disgusted.

Ellis sighed and sat down beside her. "They're having sex. It's what married couples do over here when they want to have a baby."

She frowned. "But why are these people doing it in front of a camera?"

He cleared his throat as if he was uncomfortable with the conversation. "Because it's fun. And because people like to watch it."

Kaitlyn turned to meet his eyes once more and found a surprising mixture of emotions in them. "Do people always make a video when they do it?"

His mouth curled in amusement at her question. "No. Most people just do it in private."

"And what's their reason for doing it?"

He shrugged. "It feels good."

Kaitlyn looked back at the screen, noting how much the people in the video seemed to be enjoying what they were doing.

Another thought occurred to her and she quickly turned back to him. "Have you done this?"

Ellis eyed her silently for a few seconds and then slowly nodded his head.

"Oh my god."

She suddenly felt like she didn't know the man in front of her at all.

How was it possible for her friend to have changed so much when she was practically still the same person she was thirteen years ago when he left?

She wanted to ask who he'd done it with, but then decided she would prefer not to know because just the idea of him being naked with a woman sent a sickening wave of jealousy through her, unlike anything she'd ever experienced before.

Quickly shutting the laptop, she put it down on the bed and moved away from both it and him.

"Can we go back downstairs now?" she asked quietly.

Ellis's gaze burned with unknown feelings as he watched her silently for a moment.

He opened his mouth briefly as if he wanted to say something but then soon snapped it shut and stood up from the bed, avoiding looking in her direction.

"Yeah, okay. Let's go."

Chapter Twenty Two

Kaitlyn did her best to not speak to Ellis for the rest of the time she was at the house.

She purposely didn't sit next to him when they were eating and she kept her gaze focused on either her food or Nicholas and Angela as much as possible.

There was only the odd time when the conversation required her eyes to stray to him, but in each instance he always seemed to be deliberately looking away from her.

She couldn't make the memory of the video disappear from her brain, and each time an image came to the forefront of her mind, she suddenly imagined Ellis doing the same things with a faceless woman.

How was she supposed to act normal around him after finding out he did something like that?

How was she ever supposed to look at him without picturing him wrapped around a woman's naked body?

When the time came for her to leave, she hugged Angela and Nicholas goodbye and was hoping to escape having to do the same with Ellis when Angela suddenly spoke.

"You can't walk home by yourself, love. It's dark. Ellis can walk you home again."

Kaitlyn's eyes immediately flashed over to him, seeing the hesitation in his expression, but he must have realised that Angela wouldn't have allowed him to refuse because he sighed quietly and went to put on his coat before opening the front door.

"After you."

Kaitlyn gave Angela and Nicholas one final smile and a promise to try and see them soon before stepping outside and marching off down the street as quickly as possible in the hopes that she could make the journey as short as possible and could avoid having to make conversation on the way.

"Slow down," Ellis called from behind her, jogging to catch up. "Why are you in such a rush?"

"I'm cold. I want to get home and get warm."

He chose not to acknowledge the lie and instead seemed to want to wind her up further. "Do you want my jacket?"

She shot him a look of disbelief and his mouth curved in amusement before he suddenly turned serious. "Do you hate me now?"

Kaitlyn stared straight ahead. "I don't hate you. I just feel weird around you."

"That's understandable." He sighed. "I'm sorry. I wish I'd never said anything."

She scoffed. "I wish I'd never asked."

Ellis came to a sudden standstill and she stopped too, wondering what he was doing.

"Kaitlyn," he started, pushing his hands deep into his pockets as he shifted his feet nervously. "There's so much I want to explain to you."

"What do you mean?"

"There's things I wish I could make you understand. I hate that you're disgusted with me right now for something that would be completely normal to anyone else. I hate that you're always trying to put a distance between us. And I hate that you stopped our kiss the other night when I *know* you were enjoying it."

"Stop mentioning it!" Kaitlyn shouted, outraged.

"I'm sorry! I just need you to realise that things like that aren't bad. You don't have to feel guilty"

He surprised her by suddenly cupping her face in his hands, making her cheeks tingle where his skin touched hers. "It's okay if you liked it," he murmured. "And it's okay if you want it to happen again."

"Don't," she said weakly.

"I won't," he promised. "I'm not gonna rush you."

Kaitlyn didn't exactly understand what he meant by that but she allowed herself to relax, knowing that he wasn't going to catch her off guard and kiss her again.

"Come on," he said softly, dropping his hands from her face and taking a step back. "Let's get you home."

They walked the rest of the way in silence until they were finally outside her house, looking up at the bedroom window she'd climbed out of earlier.

"Do you think your mum has realised you left?" he asked her as she tried to figure out how she was going to climb back up.

Kaitlyn shook her head. "She's not called me or anything so I think I actually managed to get away with it. If she knew I'd probably have a hundred missed calls and there'd be a search party out looking for me." She smiled widely at the thought and he mirrored her amusement.

"Okay," he said, looking between her and the still open window. "I'll give you a leg up."

She raised her eyebrows. "Seriously?"

"Yeah, it's the only way you're getting back inside without anyone noticing or hearing."

Knowing that he was right she sighed reluctantly and then got herself into position, placing her leg on his linked hands when he offered them to her.

"Are you ready?" he asked, looking as if he found the whole situation hilarious.

She nodded.

"One, two, three, go!"

She used the wall to push herself up at the same time as he raised his hands to give her more momentum until she could finally grasp hold of the edge of the windowsill.

"What am I supposed to do now?" she whisper shouted as she dangled from the window ledge with only his hands beneath her feet keeping her from falling.

Without warning, he suddenly jumped up and pushed his hands against her bottom, forcing her half way through the window before he then did the same move again and pushed her the rest of the way until she landed clumsily on her bedroom floor.

She was so shocked by the unexpectedness of it, and by the fact that he'd touched her there that it took her a few moments to recover and manage to stand up.

Leaning her head out of the window, she saw Ellis still standing below. "Err, thank you," she said quietly.

His lips quirked in a half smile. "No problem." Reaching into his jeans pocket, he pulled out his phone and then looked up at her expectantly. "Can I have your number?"

"Um, yeah, okay." She recited it to him and watched him add it to his contacts.

"Are you working tomorrow?" he asked, seeming unwilling to go home just yet.

Kaitlyn shook her head. "It's my day off."

"Will you come to the house then? For about one 'o' clock? We're gonna start clearing out grandma's things. You could help, if you want?"

She took a moment to think about it, wondering if it was a good idea. Her only plan for her day off had been to go for a walk like usual and then maybe go home and read, so the idea of having company did sound a lot more appealing; and she knew her parents would both be out all day.

"Okay, yeah. I'll come and help," she told him, causing him to grin widely.

"Cool." She liked the warm look in his eyes as he gazed up at her. "Goodnight then, Kaitlyn. I'll see you tomorrow."

"Goodnight Ellis."

She closed her window once he'd walked away and then tried to be as silent as possible as she went to have a wash before climbing in bed.

She spent a while staring up at her ceiling, feeling too awake from the adrenalin of the evening to go to sleep yet, when her phone suddenly chimed from the bedside table.

Reaching over, she saw she'd received a text from an unknown number, but when she opened it she smiled when she realised it was a message from Ellis.

Now you have my number too :) Have a good sleep. I already can't wait to see you tomorrow xx

As she rolled over and shut her eyes, she repeated his words over and over in her mind, feeling as if something new and exciting had started between the two of them, even though she wasn't exactly sure what it was or where it would lead.

All she knew was that she was eager to find out.

Chapter Twenty Three

Kaitlyn's parents left early the next day; her dad going to work at the office and her mum going to help some volunteers at the church with tidying the gardens there.

She told her parents that she would probably go for a walk in the afternoon so might not be home when they got in, and they accepted her story easily, having no reason to doubt her after twenty six years of her following their every order.

Kaitlyn spent the morning reading and then left earlier than planned to go to see Ellis, Nicholas and Angela, both because she didn't have anything else to do but also because she was looking forward to seeing them all again; Ellis especially.

A small voice in her mind wondered how she was going to cope when the family had to go home to New York, but she forced the thought away and told herself to only worry about it when the time came.

Ellis opened the door when she arrived, smiling widely when he saw her.

"You're early," he noted.

"Yeah. Sorry."

He laughed. "You don't need to apologise. We like having you here."

Kaitlyn followed him into the house, finding Nicholas and Angela sitting in the living room, both looking pleased to see her as well.

"Hi love," Angela said, standing up to hug her. Kaitlyn had the sudden realisation that she'd received more affection from the woman in the past few days than she had from her mum in *years*. "Thanks for agreeing to help us today."

"No worries, err what would you like me to do?"

Ellis jumped in to answer before his mum could. "You can help me clear out the loft," he said. "If you don't mind."

"Umm, yeah, okay." Kaitlyn quickly glanced at Angela to check that she was alright with the plan.

"Yeah that's fine," the older woman said. "Me and Nicholas can start in the basement."

Kaitlyn still found it strange that Angela didn't seem to have a problem with her son finding excuses to be alone with her, but she wasn't going to question it and instead just smiled and let Ellis lead her from the room and up the stairs where he then opened the hatch to the loft and pulled the ladders down.

"Do you want to go first?" he asked her, gesturing towards the ladders.

Kaitlyn suddenly remembered the night before when he'd helped push her into her bedroom window by placing his hands on her bottom.

"Err, no it's okay. You can."

He swiftly climbed the ladders in only a matter of seconds and she followed slowly behind him, being careful to hold on tightly and watch her feet as she took each step up so that she wouldn't lose her balance.

"Are you still scared of heights?" he asked, sounding amused as he watched her slow approach. "I would have thought the fact you managed to sneak out of your bedroom last night meant you'd got over your fear."

She would have thought the same thing, but a ladder was a lot more unstable than the wall she'd climbed down and this time she didn't have the adrenaline rush of knowing she could get caught out at any moment.

When she finally made it up, she crawled a few paces across the wooden floor to make sure that she was well clear of the opening before she had the guts to get to her feet.

"Wow," she said as she slowly looked around at the room crammed full of boxes. "I think this is gonna take more than just an afternoon."

Ellis laughed. "I know. Why do you think we've planned to stay here for six weeks? The basement's just as bad. We never realised grandma was such a hoarder."

Kaitlyn felt overwhelmed to see how much rubbish had been squashed in the reasonably small space. Boxes were piled high, overflowing with different ornaments and bits of paper, and there were random objects scattered around the floor as if Ethel had literally just thrown them up there instead of putting them away properly.

She gave Ellis a look of disbelief but then asked, "So, where should we start?"

Chapter Twenty Four

In the end, they cleared a space on the floor so that they had room to sit down, and then Ellis collected boxes from the piles one by one which they would then look through together to decide what could be kept, thrown away or given to charity.

"What's this?" Kaitlyn asked, pulling a handful of broken paintbrushes out of one of the boxes. "Why would she keep these?"

Ellis responded by holding up a statue of a rat striking a strange pose. "Why would she keep this?"

They both burst out laughing and then began a sort of game of trying to find the strangest thing they could out of Ethel's possessions.

"I think she must have kept the wrapping paper from every gift she ever received," Ellis said, looking through a box full of the stuff; some looking bright and almost new whilst other pieces were worn and yellowing as if they were a couple of decades old.

Kaitlyn laughed and reached for the next box, feeling her eyes light up when she saw what was inside. "Oh look! Pictures!"

Ellis moved to sit even closer beside her so they could look together.

The first pack was photos of Ethel and her husband who had died many years ago, before Kaitlyn had even met the family. Another packet had the couple with Angela when she was a baby and then as she grew older, and there were some photos of Angela with Kaitlyn's mum, smiling and with their arms wrapped around each other, looking like the best friends they used to be.

The packets further down in the box had pictures of Nicholas and Ellis when they were first born and throughout their childhood, abruptly stopping once they reached their mid teens and had to move away.

"My dad," Ellis said with a soft smile on his face as she stared at a photo of him, his brother and both their parents. "This must have been taken not long before he died."

Kaitlyn took the picture from him, examining the handsome man who had so many similar features to his son. She'd only met Dennis a handful of times before he'd died from cancer when Ellis had been eight and Nicholas was ten.

"You all look so happy," she noted as she gazed at the picture of the family. A thought occurred to her and she went quiet for a moment before saying, "I don't think me and my mum and dad have ever looked this happy together."

She met Ellis's eyes and they exchanged a sad smile before she suddenly felt the urge to start apologising again.

"I really am sorry for what I said about Nicholas that day," she told him. "I know I can't just blame it on my mum, but when I'd been raised to believe that being gay was wrong, I didn't even think to try and make my own opinion on the matter, and I kind of just thought that what everyone else was saying must be right. Does that make sense?"

Ellis nodded calmly. "It's fine. Don't worry about it. You've already apologised and I understand why you said it all."

"But it ruined everything between us," she reminded him, as if he didn't already know. "We could have stayed in contact this whole time but because I said that stupid stuff it made you want nothing to do with me."

Ellis reached out and placed a comforting hand over hers, causing a jolt to run through her skin. "Forget about it," he told her. "We've got the chance to fix things now. And don't blame yourself for what happened between us that day. It was just as much my fault as it was yours."

"What do you mean?"

He sighed. "I think I purposely overreacted to what you said because I thought it would be easier to hate you than to have to deal with missing you." He let out a sardonic laugh. "But it didn't even work. I still thought about you all the time."

Kaitlyn smiled. "I thought about you all the time too."

"Good." He gave her hand a slight squeeze. "I have to admit, when I found out grandma had died I was sad, of course, but I also thought about you straight away and I was glad it gave me a reason to come here and see you again."

"I thought the same thing." She frowned when she realised something still didn't make sense to her. "But why did you seem so hostile when you looked at me at the funeral? I thought it meant that you still hated me."

At that, he looked embarrassed. "I thought you'd hate us. I thought you'd have grown up to be just like your mum and all the others, so I didn't think you'd want to give me the time of day."

Kaitlyn gazed at him silently, thinking about what he'd said and about how people's prejudices had made her lose him from her life for so many years.

She wondered where they'd both be now if their rift hadn't happened.

Examining his kind, handsome face, she knew she would have still been attracted to him, but that it would have probably been a lot more awkward to have to switch between being friends to whatever they were at the moment.

In that sense, their time apart could almost be seen as a good thing; but she knew in an instant that she didn't want distance between them anymore.

"I'm not like my mum," she told him. "I don't want to be like any of the people around here."

"I know," Ellis said quietly.

But Kaitlyn didn't think her words were enough. She needed to *show* him just how serious she was.

Moving up to rest on her knees, she locked eyes with him intently. "I'm not gonna let other people's opinions control what I do with my life from now on," she told him in a voice she barely recognised as belonging to her.

Then, tentatively wrapping her arms around his neck, she leaned down and placed her mouth on his.

Chapter Twenty Five

Ellis responded immediately, pressing his lips more firmly against hers as he ran his hands down her spine and grasped hold of her waist.

Kaitlyn let him lead the kiss, being careful to move her mouth in the same way as him until she was finally able to relax enough to just do whatever felt natural.

When he slipped his tongue in her mouth, she was still shocked like she had been the last time, but she quickly recovered and let her eyes fall closed once she realised how strangely good it felt to have their tongues twisting together.

An unexpected moan escaped from her throat, causing her to gasp against his mouth momentarily before he quickly reconnected their lips and began to lean her back until she was lay down on the wooden floor with his heavy form on top of her.

Kaitlyn felt his warm hands start to roam up and down her body and she allowed herself to feel him in the same way, enjoying the quiet noises he made which told her that he liked it as she stroked her fingers over his chest and down towards the bottom of his t-shirt.

He abruptly pulled back and she worried that the kiss was already over, but then smiled when she realised he was just moving his lips to her neck to begin kissing her there.

The sensations it caused in her body were incredible and she squirmed beneath him as she felt herself losing control.

"Kaitlyn," Ellis murmured, moving his head back up and gazing deeply into her eyes. She was surprised to see how much his had darkened and she wondered if hers looked the same.

"Ellis," she said in barely more than a whisper.

His mouth came down urgently on hers once more and he'd just tangled his fingers through her hair to hold her close to him when she suddenly became aware of something hard digging into her lower stomach.

"What's that?" she asked, pulling away slightly. "Do you have something in your pocket?"

Ellis's expression suddenly changed and he quickly looked down and shifted his hips so that the object wasn't pressing against her anymore.

"It's nothing," he told her nervously. "It's just what happens when a guy gets...excited."

Kaitlyn frowned at him but, remembering the video that she'd seen the day before, she decided to not ask any more.

Apparently wanting to change the subject, Ellis stroked her hair back from her forehead and stared into her eyes in a way that felt intimate. "That was nice," he murmured.

She nodded in agreement. "Yeah it was."

His lips curled up in a soft smile. "I'm glad you're not freaking out this time," he said, causing her to blush. "Does that mean you'll be okay if I kiss you again sometime?"

Kaitlyn couldn't help but giggle. "Yeah, that should be alright."

"Good. But I warn you now, I might want to kiss you *a lot*."

A fluttering sensation started in her chest and, in that moment, she felt as if the future that had always been planned out for her had been re-written.

"You can kiss me as much as you like."

Chapter Twenty Six

They spent another hour going through boxes in the loft until Angela finally called up the stairs to tell them to stop for the day.

Ellis went down the ladders first, taking the box of photos they'd found with him to show his family, before he then held his arms up to help guide Kaitlyn down.

A thrill ran through her when she felt his hands on her hips and once her feet had touched the floor, she turned to smile at him, receiving an unexpected peck on the lips.

It amazed her to see how casual Ellis was about an act such as kissing, and she wondered if she'd be the same once she had a bit more experience with it. Already she felt more comfortable around him even though she would have thought she'd have the opposite reaction after finally being intimate with someone.

"I'm gonna go to the toilet," she told him as he made to walk downstairs.

"Okay. I'll meet you down there."

She only took a minute and was soon going down to join him and the others in the kitchen where she could hear them talking, but she came to a halt at the bottom of the stairs when she heard Angela say her name.

More specifically, she said, "Is something going on between you and Kaitlyn?"

Kaitlyn waited to see how Ellis would respond, having not had a chance to discuss what they were going to tell people yet.

"What do you mean?" he asked his mum, sounding cautious.

"Well, I know how close you both used to be when you were younger, and I saw how devastated you were after we had to leave. I always suspected you wanted to be more than just friends with her and that you probably would have ended up together if we hadn't had to move away, so I was just wondering if any of your old feelings had returned now that we're back here?"

Ellis was quiet for a few moments before he asked, "Would it be bad if there *was* something going on between us?"

Angela didn't get a chance to reply before Nicholas spluttered, "Of course it would be bad!"

"Why?"

99

"Things are different here, Ellis," Nicholas said, speaking to him as though he was a child. "You can't just have sex with her and then leave in a few weeks like you usually do with all your other women. Her reputation would be ruined and it would affect her for the rest of her life whilst you just carry on with your life in New York. It wouldn't be fair."

Kaitlyn's blood ran cold as she struggled to digest everything Nicholas had just said.

The reminder that they would all be going home to America in less than a month was painful after the kiss she'd shared with Ellis upstairs, and tears filled her eyes as she realised that she had to face the reality that whatever was going on between them could never be forever.

Nicholas was right.

She shouldn't give Ellis her innocence when he was just going to leave her alone again and she would one day have to find another husband.

But it was Nicholas's other words which bothered her the most.

Before she'd seen the videos on Ellis's laptop she wouldn't have understood what sex was, but now that she knew, she could easily figure out what Nicholas had meant when he talked about all the other women Ellis did it with at home and then left.

She suddenly realised just how little she must mean to him. When she'd been considering each moment with him as special, he'd just been doing something to entertain himself whilst he was on holiday.

It made her feel dirty and used, and she was disgusted with herself for ever letting him touch her.

As the first tear fell down her cheek, she quickly wiped it away, knowing she had to compose herself and walk into the kitchen to join them.

She took a deep breath and made her way into the room, cutting their conversation off just as Ellis looked to be about to reply to his brother.

"Oh, hello dear. I was wondering where you'd got to," Angela said with a smile as they all turned to look at her.

Kaitlyn looked between them, wondering how they could all seem so casual after what they had just been discussing. It made her wonder what else they'd said about her when she wasn't around.

"Ellis was just showing us the pictures you found," Nicholas told her, pushing out a chair and gesturing for her to sit down to join them.

"I'm gonna go home," she said bluntly, knowing she wouldn't be able to hold her tears back for much longer, and wanting to get away from the three of them after what she'd heard.

"Already?" Ellis asked, sounding disappointed.

She forced herself to meet his eyes. "Yeah, my mum will be home soon."

"Oh, okay. I'll walk you back then."

As he moved towards her she put a hand up to stop him. "No, it's alright. I probably shouldn't be seen walking with you when it's daylight."

Ellis's face fell and his probing eyes began to examine her face as if he was trying to figure out the reason behind her sudden change of mood.

Kaitlyn saw the moment when he must have realised she'd overheard them all talking because his expression became fearful and his whole body tensed.

She turned away from him, not wanting to give him any more of her attention, and went to hug Angela goodbye.

"Come back anytime you like," the older woman told her. "As you've probably figured out, we need all the help we can get clearing this place out."

Kaitlyn gave her an awkward smile, honestly not knowing at that moment if she would want to come back to the house again.

"Bye Nicholas," she said, giving him a quick one armed hug and then ignoring Ellis all together as she strutted out of the kitchen, moving quickly towards the front door.

Just before she closed it behind her she heard Ellis shouting at his mum and brother.

"She fucking heard you!"

Chapter Twenty Seven

Kaitlyn wasn't particularly surprised when she heard pounding footsteps chasing after her before she'd even managed to turn off the street, but she rolled her eyes to herself, wishing Ellis would leave her alone, before she reluctantly turned to face him.

"Kaitlyn," he said desperately, coming to a stop in front of her.

She interrupted before he could continue. "Go away Ellis. Don't try to explain yourself to me because it won't work. I don't want to hear any more about the other girls you've been with, and I don't need any excuses from you."

"But it's not like that with you," he started, but again she held a hand up to stop him.

"It doesn't matter. Regardless of that, Nicholas was right. You'll be going home in a few weeks so it would be stupid for us to get involved. I'm not going to let you ruin me."

"I don't want to ruin you!" Ellis protested. "I just want-"

She raised her eyebrows when he stopped talking mid-sentence. "What? What do you want?"

He let out a heavy sigh. "I don't know."

Kaitlyn waited for him to say more, but when he just gave her a defeated look she realised he had nothing to add.

"Well, whatever you want Ellis," she started. "Go and have it with one of your American girls."

She turned her back to him and walked away, finally letting her tears fall.

Chapter Twenty Eight

The next time Kaitlyn saw Ellis was at church.

He'd tried to contact her numerous times in the couple of days since she'd last seen him, but she'd ignored every phone call and deleted all of his apologetic texts.

When he, Angela and Nicholas walked into the church the following Sunday, she heard her mum muttering about them again, saying that it was ridiculous for the vicar to have refused to help and for them to be in a sacred place, and for once Kaitlyn didn't find herself wanting to defend them. Not because she agreed with her mother, but because she too wished they hadn't turned up.

She wondered what her mum would say if she told her about Ellis's *activities* in New York.

She'd probably want to have him exorcised.

Kaitlyn smiled to herself about her private joke, and unfortunately Ellis chose that exact moment to turn his head and lock eyes with her.

Her smile quickly fell away and she spun back around in her seat to face the front where the vicar was about to start his sermon.

Just like the previous week, Kaitlyn could feel Ellis's eyes on her throughout the entire service but she did her best to ignore it.

When the service ended, she planned to stay close to her parents and leave the church with them so that Ellis wouldn't try to ambush her again, but her plan turned out to be pointless when she suddenly heard Angela's familiar voice speaking from beside her.

"Hello Melinda," she said, addressing Kaitlyn's mum. "How've you been?"

Melinda looked outraged. "Don't talk to me!" she said, purposely being as loud as possible in order to draw attention. "We're not friends anymore."

Angela remained calm. "Doesn't that seem a bit silly to you? I was hoping you and your family might want to come to my house for some lunch. We could have a catch up." She caught Kaitlyn's eyes and smiled but Kaitlyn looked away.

Melinda laughed mockingly. "I hope you're joking? I wouldn't want to be seen dead with the likes of you!"

By that point, she had a crowd of people behind her, waiting to back her up and throw their own insults.

Angela looked around them all and appeared to realise her efforts were fruitless because she started backing away with a sad look on her face.

"Okay. Never mind."

Kaitlyn felt awful, and she was just considering the consequences of apologising on behalf of her mum when they all suddenly heard shouting from outside the church.

"You're not wanted here!" a masculine voice was saying.

When another man's voice replied, Kaitlyn immediately recognised it as Nicholas's and she saw the worry appear on Angela's face before she ran off towards the front doors.

"What's going on?" A voice murmured behind Kaitlyn.

As one, the whole group that had been watching her mum's confrontation surged forward, wanting to see whatever spectacle was happening outside.

Kaitlyn followed slowly, with anxiety twisting her gut as she heard the shouting getting louder and Ellis's voice joining in with the argument.

"He's doing nothing wrong! None of us are!"

When she reached the front steps she could barely see through the throngs of people that were surrounding Nicholas, Ellis, Angela and a man she regularly saw at church called Michael.

"Leave us alone," Angela implored him. "We just want to go home."

"Good," Michael said. "Then go back to America."

"Don't talk to my mum like that," Nicholas told him in a warning voice, stepping towards the other man threateningly.

But Michael wasn't intimidated. "Why? What's someone like *you* going to do?"

Before Kaitlyn even saw his arm move, Nicholas suddenly punched Michael in the face, causing a collective gasp to sound from the crowd.

"Nicholas!" Angela shouted at her son. "Calm down!"

At that moment, Ellis's gaze caught Kaitlyn's and they exchanged a wide eyed look before he turned back to the man who his brother had just hit.

"Look, we're leaving okay? Just let us pass."

But Michael completely ignored Ellis's placating tone, and a small cry came out of Kaitlyn's mouth as he abruptly launched his own fists towards Nicholas, striking him with a dull thud.

"Oh my god," she said, automatically pushing through the crowd without even thinking about what she was doing.

When she reached the group, Nicholas was holding his jaw, Angela looked horrified, and Ellis had positioned himself between the two men to stop any more fighting.

A quick glance at Michael's expression showed that he was very proud of what he'd done and, by the gleeful looks of the crowd, they were too.

"Are you okay?" Kaitlyn asked Nicholas as she placed a comforting hand on his arm.

But her mother's hand suddenly appeared to slap it away. "Kaitlyn! Don't touch him! What are you doing?"

"Mum! Get off me." For once she tried to fight against her mother, but Melinda just dug her nails into her arms, refusing to let go.

"Kaitlyn, listen to your mother!" her dad's booming voice suddenly said from beside her, surprising her with the amount of authority she heard in his tone.

Kaitlyn looked at him in shock.

Her dad had never spoken to her like that before. He'd never taken charge of a situation and had always let her mother speak for him. She'd always wondered if he was secretly on her side and that, if the time came for it, he would stick up for her instead of his wife.

But she realised in that moment that he was just as bad as her mum.

No one was on her side.

Feeling numb from the realisation of just how alone she was in the world, she didn't protest when her parents pulled her away from the scene, holding her tightly between them the entire time they marched her home.

Chapter Twenty Nine

Later that night, Kaitlyn snuck out of her window again, planning to do what she'd done before and race across town to see Angela and the others.

She needed to see that Nicholas was okay.

She needed to do something rebellious after the show her parents had made of her outside the church.

And, against common sense, she *wanted* to see Ellis.

She was still angry and hurt by the things she'd found out about him and other women, and she still knew that things between them wouldn't be able to go any further due to the fact he was going to be leaving, but she couldn't bear the thought of not at least keeping in contact with him as friends this time.

She wanted him in her life.

She wanted the whole family in her life.

When she reached the house and knocked on the door, no one came to answer it which she thought was unusual.

She knocked again, loudly, and a moment later Ellis's voice asked, "Who is it?"

Kaitlyn frowned. "It's me," she announced.

The door quickly swung open and Ellis stared down at her with a wide grin. "Kaitlyn, you came back."

"I wanted to see how Nicholas was after what happened before."

Ellis's smile fell and he stepped aside, letting her into the house without another word. She knew she'd disappointed him but she told herself she would fix things between them later.

Walking into the living room, she found Angela and Nicholas sitting on the couch.

"Oh my god," Kaitlyn said when she noticed the large bruise on Nicholas's jaw. "Are you alright?"

He scoffed. "I suppose." His expression quickly softened and he gazed into her eyes earnestly. "Thank you for what you did earlier. I know it must have been hard for you to try and stick up for yourself against your parents."

Kaitlyn scowled at the memory. "It didn't work though."

Nicholas smiled sadly. "It still means a lot."

Angela stood up to give Kaitlyn a hug and then she rested her hand on her shoulder affectionately.

"It means a lot that you came back to see us as well," she said. "I know we all upset you the other day."

Kaitlyn felt her cheeks heat at the reminder. "It wasn't you that upset me," she said. "It was just the things I heard."

At that, Angela looked between her sons who seemed to be locked in some kind of angry staring contest.

Nicholas sighed. "I'm sorry, Kaitlyn. I shouldn't have said those things." He stood up and stared directly into her eyes as his tone became serious. "Please don't fall out with my brother over what I said. He really cares about you. You're not like the other girls he's dated in the past, and I should have realised that before I opened my big mouth and upset you."

"Yeah, you should have," Ellis told him gruffly.

"It's okay Nicholas," Kaitlyn said. "I know you were just trying to protect me, and I appreciate that." She settled her eyes on Ellis. "Can we go upstairs and talk?"

Chapter Thirty

Once they were in his bedroom and away from his mum and brother, Ellis came up behind Kaitlyn and wrapped his arms around her waist, leaning down to kiss her neck softly.

"Are we okay now?" he murmured against her skin.

She pulled out of his embrace. "I don't know."

"But didn't you hear what Nicholas said?" he protested. "The other girls I've been with never meant anything to me. It's *you* I've always wanted to be with."

"You have?"

He nodded and stepped forward to take hold of her hand. "I didn't realise just how strongly I felt about you until we left for America, but since then you've always been on my mind. At first I convinced myself there was still hope for us, but then I had to resign myself to the fact I might never see you again, so that's why I started messing around with all those other girls."

Kaitlyn searched his face and his words for any hint of a lie, but found only the truth.

She remembered what she'd heard Angela saying in the kitchen before Nicholas had dropped his unexpected revelation, and she wondered if perhaps other people had thought she and Ellis would get together one day; at least until everything had gone wrong and he'd had to leave.

Back then, she'd never considered him ever being anything other than her friend, but as she looked at him standing in front of her and remembered what it was like to have him kiss her, she knew that being friends wouldn't be enough like she'd thought.

She wanted *everything* with him.

But there was just one problem.

She could forget about his past with other girls because she believed what he'd said about them meaning nothing, but there was still one obstacle standing in her way.

In that instant she made a decision.

"Do you really want to be with me?" she asked him.

"Of course." his thumb began to stroke the back of her hand.

"And you're sure you won't change your mind?"

Ellis cracked a smile. "If I've not changed my mind in thirteen years, I doubt I'll change it now."

Kaitlyn licked her lips nervously and then stared him straight in the eye. "Take me home with you then. Take me to New York."

Chapter Thirty One

Ellis watched her warily, as if he wasn't sure whether she was being serious. "Do you really mean that?"

Kaitlyn nodded firmly. There wasn't a doubt in her mind now that she'd made her decision.

"I don't want to live here anymore," she told him. "I don't want my parents telling me what to do and who to spend time with. I need to get away from them."

Ellis still looked cautious, but as he examined her determined expression a smile gradually began to spread across his face. "You'd really leave your life here... to be with me?"

Kaitlyn felt her cheeks heat with a blush. "Yeah, is that weird?"

"Maybe to some people," he said, laughing, which only made her more embarrassed until he added, "But I'd do the same for you."

Kaitlyn smiled. "So, do you think we should go and tell your mum? Make sure it's okay with her?"

Ellis shook his head and loosened his hand from hers before trailing it up her arm so he could cup her cheek as he stared down at her intensely. "We'll tell them later," he said in a low, husky voice which sent tingles down her spine. "We'll figure everything out, but for now I just want to kiss you, okay?"

Kaitlyn gazed up at him nervously, feeling herself getting swept away by his words. "Okay." her voice shook as she spoke. "But I'm not ready to do more than just kissing yet."

Ellis stroked his thumb over her lips. "I know, we don't have to," he said softly, reassuring her. "I'm not going to rush you into anything; especially not now that I know we've got forever."

They shared an almost giddy smile and then his eyes darkened in a way that was starting to become familiar, and he brought his mouth down on hers.

Chapter Thirty Two

Kaitlyn lost herself in the kiss, wrapping her arms around Ellis's neck and reaching up on her tiptoes in order to press her lips even more firmly against his.

When he began to walk her backwards, she let him, laughing into his mouth when they both ended up toppling onto the mattress.

"Are you okay?" he asked between kisses as his hand slid down her body and stroked the strip of bare skin where her t-shirt had risen up.

Kaitlyn nodded and then took the initiative to slip her tongue into his mouth and start moving it in the same way that he'd done with her before.

Ellis let out a low moan. "God, you're getting good at this," he told her.

She giggled but then abruptly broke off when she felt something digging into her stomach again.

"Sorry," Ellis said, shifting his hips slightly off her. "I just can't help it when I'm with you like this."

"How do you make it go away?"

He met her eyes and gave her a meaningful look.

"Oh. Like, in the videos?"

"Yeah."

"Is that the only way?"

He watched her carefully. "No, it will just go away on its own after a while. But, I can make it go away myself."

"How?"

He cleared his throat. "Err, I'm not sure you'd want to know." When she just raised her eyebrows, waiting for more of an explanation, he continued. "If I...stroke it...it will go down."

Kaitlyn almost laughed at just the thought of it. He made it sound like some kind of genie lamp.

But her curiosity got the better of her. "Will you show me?"

Ellis's eyes widened in surprise, but she noticed a hint of excitement in their depths. "Really?"

"Yeah." She began to sit up, forcing him to roll off of her body, before she crossed her legs and gazed at him expectantly. "Do it."

She watched his throat move as he swallowed. "Okay."

Sitting back against his headboard, he undid his jeans and began to pull them down.

Kaitlyn held her breath as a strange sensation started in her lower body and the air around them seemed to get heavier.

Once Ellis pulled his boxers down to his knees, leaving his groin area completely bare, she stared in fascination at the large body part he'd revealed. It was protruding upwards intimidatingly, reflecting what she'd seen from the men on his videos, and she found herself unable to take her eyes off of it, even when she felt Ellis watching her, trying to judge her reaction.

"Go on then," she urged him in a whisper. "Stroke it."

A strange groan ripped out of his throat and his hand quickly wrapped around the base of his...*thing* before he began to move it up and down in a steady rhythm.

The room was completely silent other than the sound of his hand moving against himself and the odd panting sound that he made.

Kaitlyn flicked her eyes up to his face and saw that he was staring at her intently, biting his lip as his hand gradually began to move faster.

"Does that feel good?" she asked him, seeing the obvious look of pleasure on his face.

He shut his eyes for a moment and a breath hissed out from between his teeth. "Fuck, don't say that to me. You don't know how good it sounds." His eyes locked back on hers. "Yes, it feels good. It feels amazing when I know you're watching me."

Kaitlyn blushed and then a sudden urge came over her and she moved her hand almost involuntarily, circling her fingers around him just above where his own hand was.

"Shit," Ellis panted, letting his own hand fall away in an obvious signal for her to take over.

His eyes were almost completely black and she had to look away from the intensity of them before she slowly began to slide her hand along him in the way she'd seen him do, glancing back at him every now and then to make sure that she was doing it right.

"Is that okay?"

Ellis's face twisted almost painfully. "More than okay. Please don't stop."

She started to go faster, mesmerised when she watched his head fall back against the headboard as his chest began to move up and down rapidly.

"That's it Kaitlyn," he told her. "Fuck, you're gonna make me come."

She didn't understand what that meant until his whole body suddenly stiffened and she felt a wetness on her hand. She looked down to see that some kind of liquid was shooting out of him.

Thankfully, it wasn't urine.

As she removed her hand off his thing, it flopped down between his legs, now soft, and she looked from it to him where he was lying with his eyes still closed, seemingly trying to get control of his breathing.

"Are you alright?"

He nodded.

"Err, what should I do with this?" She held up her hand to show him the mess once he'd opened his eyes again and he let out a laugh.

"Um, here." He reached for a box of tissues beside his bed and started to try and clean the strange white liquid off of her. "You should probably go and wash the rest off."

Kaitlyn couldn't help but laugh as well, even though she didn't properly understand what had happened. "Yeah, okay."

Before she could stand up, Ellis stopped her by placing a hand on her thigh. "Thank you for doing that," he told her. "I know you don't want us to rush things, but I'd really like to return the favour sometime."

She didn't know what he meant, but the thought of him doing something similar to her and of her allowing him to touch her in such an intimate place made her mouth go dry and the muscles between her legs clench.

Maybe she *was* ready to try more than just kissing.

Chapter Thirty Three

Once Kaitlyn had cleaned herself up, she joined Ellis back in his room and they lay down side by side on his bed, staring into each other's eyes and only talking every now and then.

Mostly they just touched.

Ellis stroked his fingers through her hair, untangling all the knots and making her scalp tingle, and she in turn ran her hand across his chest and down his firm torso, feeling the hard muscles underneath his t-shirt.

"You're so beautiful," he murmured to her at one point.

She gave him a shy smile and traced her finger over his eyelids and down his nose, landing on the silver ring there. "So are you." She pulled on it. "I really like this, by the way."

He smirked. "Yeah? Good."

A thought suddenly occurred to her. "Do loads of girls say that to you?"

"Don't think about them. They don't matter."

She knew he was avoiding having to give her a real answer but didn't press the issue further, instead just asking, "How long have you had it?"

"Since I was nineteen."

Moving her hand down to his forearm, she let her finger trace the patterns of the tattoo on his left arm. "What about this?"

He looked down, following the trail she was making with his eyes. "I did this one myself last year. But the one on my right arm I got my mate to do when I first started work five years ago."

"And the one on your back?" she asked, remembering how he'd mentioned he had one there as well.

"My mate did that about three years ago."

"Can I see it?"

Ellis watched her for a moment and then slowly sat up and peeled off his t-shirt, revealing his bare chest before he twisted around to show her the tattoo between his shoulder blades.

It was some kind of circular symbol filled with swirling patterns and things that she couldn't decipher. It had been coloured in with different shades of blue, purple, orange and green, making it look both pretty and masculine.

"Cool," Kaitlyn said, touching the warm skin of his back so she could run her fingers over it. She felt his muscles tense but sensed that it was in a good way.

"I designed it myself," he told her. "It represents freedom and independence."

She laughed. "Maybe I should get one then."

He turned his head to look at her over his shoulder and raised his eyebrow. "I can do it for you, if you like? I've got my equipment here."

She was so surprised by the offer that she took a moment to think of what to say. "How is it even done?"

Ellis got up off the bed to search through his chest of drawers, pulling out a small, transparent, satchel like bag and bringing it over for her to see.

"Eww it's full of needles!" she said, moving away from it as if one of them might stab her.

Ellis laughed. "Yeah, that's how the ink gets into your skin."

"Gross." Kaitlyn had always been afraid of needles. "Why do you even have this stuff with you?"

He rolled up the bottom of his jeans, revealing his calf where there was a half finished tribal looking tattoo. "I've been working on this," he said, examining it. "Not quite sure what I want to do with it yet so I'm waiting for inspiration to hit me."

She eyed the bag of needles warily. "Well, when it does, make sure I'm not around." She looked back at him to find him watching her with an amused expression. "What?"

He shook his head. "Nothing. You're just cute."

Kaitlyn rolled her eyes, enjoying being able to joke around with him after things had been so uncomfortable between them when he'd first come back. "Thanks."

They decided to go back downstairs shortly afterwards, wanting to tell Angela and Nicholas about the plan for Kaitlyn to move to America with them.

"What if they tell me I can't come?" she asked, gripping onto his hand tightly as he led her down the stairs.

"They won't."

She hoped he was right, but knew she wouldn't be able to relax until she'd heard the words from his mum and brother herself.

As they walked towards the living room, Kaitlyn instinctively tried to pull her hand away from his but he refused to let her go. "They won't care," he assured her.

She saw that he was right when they entered the room and Angela smiled warmly at them both. "I'm guessing you two have made up?" Nicholas chuckled from his space in the corner.

"We've done more than that," Ellis said, causing his mum to frown and his brother to snort.

"Too much information dude. We don't need to know about that."

"Shut up." Ellis glared at him. "That's not what I meant."

Kaitlyn flushed and tried to hide behind his body once she realised what Nicholas had meant, but Ellis just wrapped a comforting arm around her shoulders and pulled her back beside him.

"Kaitlyn's gonna come back to America with us," he announced, causing Angela's eyebrows to raise to almost her hairline.

"Do you mean, for a holiday?"

Kaitlyn looked down at her feet, avoiding her eyes and letting Ellis do all the talking for them.

"Nope," he said proudly. "Permanently."

"Really?" Angela looked concerned and it made Kaitlyn's enthusiasm immediately disappear. "I'm not saying that because I don't want you to come," the older woman reassured her. "I'm just worried that you might regret the decision once you get there and start missing your family."

Nicholas scoffed. "Have you *met* her family? Can you blame her for wanting to leave?"

"True," Angela said before fixing her eyes back on Kaitlyn. "But are you not worried about what your mother's going to say? I wouldn't be surprised if she disowned you once you tell her."

"I don't care," Kaitlyn said, even though part of her secretly still did. "I'm doing it whether she likes it or not."

She looked around the group to see the impressed looks on Nicholas's and Ellis's faces, whilst Angela just watched her silently, looking as if she was trying to read her mind.

"Alright," she said eventually when she must have not found any doubt in Kaitlyn's expression. "I guess we need to get you a passport then."

Chapter Thirty Four

"I can't believe this is really going to happen," Ellis said as he walked her home later that night. There were no other people around so he was able to hold her hand, squeezing it gently every now and again. "After all these years, we're really going to be together."

Kaitlyn smiled. It was still hard for her to believe that he'd had feelings for her for so long; before she'd even realised how she felt herself.

So much had changed in her life within such a short space of time that it was hard for her to imagine that she would not only be leaving the country for the first time soon, but *moving* to a different country.

But she knew Ellis was worth it.

Him, and the different kind of life he could offer her.

They'd decided to not bother rocking the boat by telling her mum about the plan just yet. The family weren't due to leave for another few weeks so they didn't see the point in causing tension before they needed to. Plus, Kaitlyn was worried that her mum might somehow try to jeopardise her passport application if she found out prematurely.

It would be annoying to still have to sneak around in order to see Ellis, but she reassured herself that it wouldn't be for long and then they could start their new life together.

When they reached her house, she began to feel sad about having to leave him, even though they had plans for her to help do more clearing out the next day.

She wondered if it was stupid for her to already depend on him so much, but was quickly reassured when he wrapped his arms around her waist and pulled her close to murmur, "I'll miss you."

"I'll miss you too," she said before joking, "Why don't you come in? I'm sure you'll fit through my window."

She was surprised when he seemed to actually consider it, looking at the wall as if he was trying to figure out the best way to climb up.

"Okay." He shrugged.

"I wasn't being serious! You can't come in. I think my mum would actually kill us both if she found you."

Instead of being put off by her words, he instead gave her a cocky smirk. "I'm willing to risk it."

Before Kaitlyn knew it, he was giving her a leg up and pushing her in using her bum as leverage like he had the last time, and then she bent over the window ledge just in time to see him awkwardly scaling the wall by using his fingertips to grip on to any small hole in the bricks whilst using his feet to bounce up the side of her house like some kind of kangaroo.

Kaitlyn was laughing hysterically by the time he landed on her bedroom carpet, smiling up at her, but they both soon froze when someone suddenly pounded on her bedroom door.

"Kaitlyn, be quiet," her mum told her sternly. "It's late. What are you laughing at?"

"Oh, sorry. I'm just watching something funny on TV."

"Well, turn it off."

With those final words, her mum stomped off down the hallway and they waited to hear the sound of her bedroom door closing before either of them was willing to risk a whisper.

"Sorry," Ellis said, still seeming like he was trying hard not to laugh. "Do you want me to leave?"

Kaitlyn looked between him and her bedroom door, wanting to tell him he was fine to stay, and knowing it was ridiculous to still be scared of her mum when she was twenty six years old, but still not wanting to get either of them in trouble when it could be so easily avoided.

"Yeah," she said with a sigh. "You probably should."

Ellis nodded understandingly. "Okay, I guess that death climb was all for nothing then," he joked teasingly.

He managed to be a lot more graceful on his way back down, and he was able to land on both feet in the soft grass in only a matter of seconds.

"See you tomorrow," he whisper shouted up to her. "I love you."

After that unexpected proclamation, he jogged off up the road, leaving Kaitlyn standing startled at her bedroom window, and unable to do anything other than watch him disappear into the darkness.

Chapter Thirty Five

Kaitlyn was still reeling from Ellis's declaration of love the next afternoon as she walked to Ethel's old house to help him and the others with more clearing out.

He'd text her earlier in the day to ask what time she finished work, but hadn't acknowledged his words from the night before or said them again so she knew it would probably be down to her to bring up the topic with him; but she was nervous about doing so.

Not because she wasn't ready to say it back, but because she'd started to convince herself that she might have misheard him and so therefore might freak him out if she told him she loved him when she saw him.

When she arrived at the house, she didn't even get a chance to knock on the door before it was suddenly flung open by Ellis who had obviously been looking out of the window for her. He pulled her inside before she could say anything and attached his mouth to hers, giving her what could only be described as a thorough kiss until she quickly pushed him away when she heard footsteps approaching them.

"Hello honey," Angela said with a smile, not seeming at all bothered about the display of affection she'd just witnessed. "Come in. I've got your passport application ready for us to go through."

Ellis took her hand and pulled her into the living room, taking away any chance of her discussing what he'd told her for the time being.

The passport form didn't take long to complete. Nicholas took a picture of her against a plain white wall and uploaded it to the computer and then she just had to answer a few simple questions and print it off to sign.

As she put her pen to the paper, she got a giddy feeling in her stomach, knowing that she was finally taking control of her own life, but it all came crashing down when she saw the final box on the form.

"Oh no," she said, reading it over and over again, hoping she might have got the words wrong. "It says one of my parents needs to sign it."

Chapter Thirty Six

"What? That can't be right," Angela said, sounding just as surprised as Kaitlyn felt.

Ellis ripped the form from her hands and read the section himself, his face turning a shade paler when he confirmed what she'd said. "Shit. This stupid fucking country! Why would a twenty six year old woman need her parents to sign a passport application?"

Nicholas looked something up on his phone. "Apparently they changed the law here a few years ago. It just applies to girls. They need either a parent, guardian or husband to sign it for them, basically to make sure that no one can leave the country to get away from their family like Kaitlyn wants to."

Ellis shook his head, seeming to be getting angrier by the second. "Unbelievable." He suddenly got an idea and turned to her with hopeful eyes. "Do you reckon your dad might do it?"

Kaitlyn gave him a sceptical look. "I doubt it after how he acted at church with my mum. He's just as bad as her."

The room went quiet as the three of them became lost in their thoughts, trying to think of a solution to the problem they faced.

"Do you think there's any way you could trick them into signing it without letting them read what it's for?" Nicholas asked, but Kaitlyn immediately shook her head, dismissing the idea, knowing her mum and dad weren't that stupid.

"Maybe you could pretend you need to leave the country for a different reason," Ellis suggested.

"Like what?"

He thought hard for about a minute before sighing in defeat. "I don't know."

They brainstormed for a while longer until Kaitlyn eventually voiced the words that she knew they all must have been thinking. "I'm not gonna be able to go with you."

"You will!" Ellis said emphatically, seeming to be trying to persuade her as much as he wanted to convince himself. "We'll figure it out."

Angela gave her a smile that didn't reach her eyes. "We will, honey. There's got to be a loophole we can find somewhere."

"And anyway," Ellis started, taking her hand and giving it a reassuring squeeze. "I'm not leaving here unless you're with me."

"Really?" Kaitlyn asked him softly, wondering if it would be selfish of her to let him stay just because she was unable to go with him.

"Of course." He leaned down to give her a quick kiss.

"Well," Nicholas suddenly said in a purposely upbeat tone. "Maybe if your mum realises it's the only way to get rid of us all, she'll agree to sign it."

Chapter Thirty Seven

"Okay, we'll see you later then" Angela said a while later as she and Nicholas were getting ready to leave to go to the cinema in the next town. They'd offered to go out in order to give Kaitlyn and Ellis some time alone for once.

"Make sure you don't just spend the whole night worrying about your passport." Angela gave Kaitlyn a warning look before she hugged her goodbye.

"I'm sure Ellis will be able to take her mind off things," Nicholas said with a sly grin, causing Kaitlyn to flush while Ellis shot his brother a warning glare.

Thankfully Angela didn't pay any attention to the innuendo.

Once they were gone, Ellis took Kaitlyn up to his room to listen to some music like they used to do when they were younger, but she was unable to switch her mind off.

"What am I gonna do?" She slumped back against his pillows dramatically.

"I don't know," Ellis said quietly from where he lay beside her. "But I promise we will think of a solution." His lips lifted slightly and he let out a small chuckle. "Even if we have to get married so that I can sign the application."

Kaitlyn forced out a laugh, ignoring the emotions that word automatically stirred up in her.

She knew Ellis was obviously not making a serious suggestion, so told herself to not get carried away.

However, him mentioning marriage did remind her of something else she needed to discuss with him.

"Ellis?"

"Yeah?"

"Um," she twisted his bed sheets between his hands nervously. "You know, when you said goodbye to me last night?" His eyes lit up with something unfamiliar. "Did you say something else after that?"

For a moment he just examined her expression, as though he was trying to figure out what she thought about his proclamation before he was willing to admit or deny it.

Kaitlyn tried to make her eyes as warm as possible, hoping he'd get the message that she wanted him to confirm it before she could risk embarrassing herself.

"Yeah, I did," he said eventually, speaking very slowly. "I didn't plan it beforehand, but I meant it. I just didn't want to bring it up again in case I'd freaked you out."

At that, she laughed, remembering how she'd worried about doing the same thing to him.

"You didn't freak me out." She paused to gather herself, wanting the words to come out perfectly because she knew she'd never get another first time saying them. "I love you, Ellis."

A broad grin stretched across his face and he suddenly dived on her, tackling her down onto the mattress so that she was trapped underneath him before he began to kiss her passionately, as if it was his way of sealing the deal.

He was breathless when he pulled away a minute or so later. "I love you too, Kaitlyn."

She didn't think she'd ever experienced happiness like the kind she'd felt in that moment and she wished there was some way she could trap the feeling inside something so she could permanently carry it around with her.

As they stared into each other's eyes like lovesick fools, letting out giddy laughs every now and again as they repeated the words to each other, a new idea suddenly came to the forefront of her brain.

"What is it?" he asked, obviously noticing some kind of change in her expression.

She sat up abruptly, forcing him to roll off of her before she surprised him by straddling his lap and wrapping her arms around his neck.

"I know what I can do," she told him, getting more excited by her idea the more she thought about it. "My parents won't want me to stay here if I embarrass them."

"Okay…"

"So, I need to ruin my reputation," she said, waiting for him to understand her plan. "And I need you to help me do it."

Chapter Thirty Eight

Ellis's eyes widened in alarm. "Do you mean...?"

Kaitlyn nodded once. "Yep. I want you to have sex with me."

She couldn't believe she was able to get the words out of her mouth so easily.

"We can't," he said, immediately sending a wave of doubt through her. "I'm not gonna let you just throw away your virginity as a way to try and force your mum to sign that application."

Kaitlyn rolled her eyes. "I wouldn't be throwing it away. I'd be giving it to you. Don't you want that?"

He sighed and tightened his hold around her waist. "Of course I do. But not until you're ready and are doing it for the right reasons."

"But I *am* ready, Ellis!" she told him forcefully, feeling even more sure of her decision now that she'd said the words out loud. "I want to give myself to you. I want to *experience* that with you."

He still looked doubtful, as if he didn't trust her to be telling the truth. "Kaitlyn, no."

But his body told a different story, and she smirked when she felt the hardness that she now recognised as being a sign of his arousal growing beneath her.

"Don't say no just because you think it's the right thing to do," she murmured. "I want this. I want you to show me what it can be like. I want to make you feel as good as I did with my hand the other day. And I want you to make me feel the same way."

He closed his eyes for a moment and she watched his jaw clench as he tried to hang on to his control, but he soon lost the fight and trailed his hand up her back to tangle in her hair as he gazed up at her with longing. "Are you sure you want it to happen like this?"

"I'm sure."

"Promise?"

Kaitlyn giggled. "Yes, I promise." As if a different person had suddenly taken over her body, making her act in a way that wasn't usual, she moved her lips to his ear and spoke in a low, breathy tone that she didn't recognise.

"Now ruin me, Ellis."

Chapter Thirty Nine

"Fuck."

Ellis quickly rolled them both over, reversing their positions so that she was beneath him once more.

"God, you have no idea how much I want you. How long I've wanted you."

He brought his mouth down to hers, slipping his tongue through her lips straight away as he grinded his hips against hers so that she could feel exactly how hard his thing was.

"Ellis," she moaned when he began trailing kisses down her neck and to her chest.

"Do you want me to stop?" he asked, still placing warm, wet kisses against her neckline.

Kaitlyn shook her head immediately. "Please don't stop."

He smiled up at her, winking teasingly before he suddenly moved up to start kissing her mouth again.

The reaction within Kaitlyn's body was new and completely unexpected. She found her hands moving in ways they never had before, without her even having to send the signal to them from her brain, and her body was rising up from the mattress of its own volition, pressing her chest against his in an effort to get as close to him as possible.

Ellis stopped for a moment when they both had to catch their breath, and he gazed down at her in wonder. "Fuck, you really want this."

She giggled. "Yeah, I really do."

The atmosphere between them changed even further with that final confirmation, and she jolted when she felt his hands reach for the bottom of her t-shirt before he slowly started to push it up her torso. Once it was around her neck, she lifted up slightly so that he could get it over her head, and then he threw the material over his shoulder as he stared intently at her bra clad chest and the breasts that were threatening to spill out of it each time she panted.

"You have a great body," he told her, swallowing nervously as his hand slowly moved to cup one of her boobs and begin to massage it. "Can I take this off as well?"

Kaitlyn nodded, licking her lips as her mouth went dry at the thought of showing him her bare chest.

His hands slid beneath her body to reach her bra clasp. She was just about to explain to him how to undo it when the material suddenly loosened around her and she realised he'd managed on his own.

"Wow, I thought you'd need help with that," she said, remembering as soon as the words came out of her mouth that he'd probably done it many times before.

Ellis met her eyes but thankfully didn't comment, so she did her best to push away the thought of him touching other girls in the same way he was touching her, and kept her eyes fixed on his as he pulled the bra away from her body.

"Fuck."

She smiled to herself, wondering how many times she was going to hear him say that word before they were done, but when his head suddenly swooped down and he latched his lips onto one of her nipples, the smile soon fell away from her face and she opened her mouth wide as she gasped in pure pleasure. "Ahhhh."

Ellis smirked against her chest and then swapped his mouth over to her other nipple, tugging on it firmly to the point where she wondered if it would leave a mark.

Whilst she was distracted by what he was doing with his tongue and lips, she felt his hands undo her jeans and was impressed when he managed to remove them without having to detach from her breasts.

He sat up to look at her once she was left in only her knickers and she immediately felt self-conscious under his heated gaze, especially when she realised that he was still fully clothed.

"Aren't you gonna get naked as well?" she asked, fighting the urge to cover herself with her hands.

Ellis smirked and began to strip, seeming to be a lot more confident with his body than she was with hers; but she couldn't blame him when she realised just how perfect he was when wearing only small black boxer shorts.

She giggled nervously as she trailed her eyes across his chest, over his abs and down to the bulge in his underwear.

"Um, what now?"

He moved down to hover over her, keeping his weight off her by resting on his elbows whilst he gazed intently into her eyes.

"If you're okay with it, I'm gonna touch you down there. It's gonna hurt at first when we have sex so I want to make sure you're properly ready for me."

Kaitlyn shifted restlessly at his words. "Okay."

He smiled reassuringly and stroked her hair back from her face. "Don't worry baby, I'm gonna make you feel good. I'm not gonna put myself inside you until after I've already made you come."

Kaitlyn frowned at the word she remembered hearing from him before. "Do you mean, like, when I touched you the other day?"

He nodded, and butterflies began in her stomach, but she found an unexpected confidence inside herself and took hold of his hand, sliding it down her stomach until it rested between her open legs.

"Touch me then. Make me...come."

Chapter Fourty

Ellis groaned loudly, in a way that almost made him sound like an animal, and the muscles in Kaitlyn's lower stomach clenched with some kind of need as he quickly removed her knickers.

She held her breath as she felt his fingers begin to probe at the sensitive flesh between her legs, and then she couldn't help but cry out when he started to stroke her in a quick, even rhythm; the same as the one he'd used when she'd watched him touch himself.

"Is that okay?" he asked in a rough voice. "Does it feel nice?"

She nodded, closing her eyes in a bid to make her feel less embarrassed about the way he was watching her so closely when she knew she must be pulling stupid faces.

"Oh my god," she gasped helplessly. "What? How? Why does it feel so good?"

Ellis chuckled above her. "It's supposed to, baby. Just enjoy it. Let it happen."

His words only helped her to start squirming more, and when he began to stroke her at an even faster pace she almost wanted to push him away because she was so worried about losing control.

"Kaitlyn, open your eyes," he told her softly.

She did as he asked, finding him staring at her hungrily, as if he was getting as much pleasure from the experience as she was, even though he wasn't being touched.

On instinct, she threw her hands up above her head to grip hold of the headboard, before she then bent her legs and raised them towards her chest, opening herself wider to him and feeling how easily his fingers slipped through her folds because of the new position.

"Fuck, you look so good like that," he told her, moving his hand even faster. "I want you to come, Kaitlyn. Do you think you're close?"

Her hips lifted slightly off the bed, pressing closer to his hand as a tightening sensation started at her core. "I think so."

"Come on baby. Come on baby. Come on baby," he began to chant.

"Oh god, oh god, oh, oh, oh-"

She detonated.

Chapter Fourty One

Even after her body had stopped shaking, it still took Kaitlyn a good couple of minutes to steady her breathing enough so that she could speak.

Ellis had moved back up the bed and was resting on his elbow at her side, watching her intently with a very cocky expression on his face.

"That was....really good," she told him, almost in disbelief. "I understand why the woman in that video was making so much noise."

He laughed. "Actually, she'll have been doing that for show to make it more entertaining to watch. The reason you were so loud is just because I'm amazing with my fingers."

Her face heated and she immediately covered it with her hands in embarrassment. "Oh my god. I'm sorry. Did I sound really stupid?"

"No, of course not." He forced her hands away from her face. "It was nice to know you were enjoying it that much."

His words reassured her. "So, will *sex* feel that good?"

"Maybe not the first time," he told her, giving her an apologetic look even though she didn't really understand why that would be the case. "But eventually it will, yeah."

Glancing down to confirm he was still hard, she brazenly wrapped her hand around him. "Can we do it now then?"

Again, he laughed, and then moved to climb back on top of her. "Are you sure you want to do this?"

"Yes!"

"Okay." He reached across to his bedside table, pulled open the drawer and got out a small box.

"What's that?" she asked, watching him take some kind of foil packet out before tossing the box to the floor.

Ellis met her eyes. "It's called a condom."

"What's it for?"

"To stop you from getting pregnant."

She frowned, having never heard that such a thing existed. "Oh."

With a mixture of curiosity and bewilderment, she kept her gaze fixed on his hands as he ripped the foil open to reveal a circular object made out of rubber, before he then rolled it on his hardness so that he was fully sheathed.

"You know the stuff that came out and got on your hands the other day?" he said, seeing her fascination. "That's the stuff that would get you pregnant so it collects it and stops it from going inside you."

Kaitlyn didn't ask any more questions because she didn't want to ruin the mood between them by starting some kind of biology lesson, and she soon forgot all about the condom anyway when Ellis brought his body down over hers so that they were face to face, with their noses so close that they were only millimetres away from touching.

She let out a small gasp when she felt his fingers slide back and forth between her legs a couple of times, as if he was checking for something, and then he asked in a low, intimate voice, "Ready?"

"Yeah."

It was scary to not know quite what was about to happen or what it would feel like, but she trusted Ellis to look after her and she was glad that he was there to share the experience with her.

She wouldn't have wanted anyone else.

"Ah." A small noise of surprise escaped from between her lips when he started to push against her *down there*, but Ellis stroked her hip reassuringly and she allowed her body to relax, spreading her legs a bit wider so that he would have more room.

Then he started pushing again, using more pressure that time as he watched what he was doing between her thighs with a look of concentration on his face.

Kaitlyn could feel her muscles stretching to accommodate him and she screwed her eyes shut as a way to stop herself from either screaming or crying from the pain; but then he was finally all the way in and he stopped moving for a few moments, giving her a chance to get used to the sensation.

"Did that hurt?" he asked, sounding worried.

She opened her eyes, giving him a sarcastic look. "Just a bit."

Chapter Fourty Two

"Tell me when I can move."

Ellis watched her intently with a small frown on his forehead, clearly worried about how much he might have hurt her.

The space between Kaitlyn's legs was still burning, but the pain had got a lot better and she knew it probably wouldn't disappear completely for a while so she might as well power through in order to get to the good stuff that Ellis had promised her would come with more experience.

"You can move," she told him, bracing herself by resting her hands on his hips.

He slid out of her and then in again experimentally, watching carefully for her reaction. She forced herself not to wince even though the movement hurt, but once he started to move more steadily she found that the pain was becoming manageable.

"Fuck," Ellis breathed out. "It feels so good to be inside you like this."

Kaitlyn kept her eyes locked on his face, enjoying seeing the way his expression changed and his eyes darkened and squinted the longer it went on for.

He checked whether she was alright or if she wanted him to stop every few seconds, but Kaitlyn found herself forgetting about how uncomfortable it was because she was just so glad to be making him feel so good.

In an effort to draw even more of a reaction from him, she wrapped her legs around his waist and moved her hips experimentally with his, causing a loud groan to rumble out of his chest.

"God, you're so tight."

He began to move even faster, and his eyes were flicking between her face and the place where they were joined together.

"Fuck, look at us," he said in amazement. "I knew we'd be so fucking good together."

When he started to chew on his lip whilst one of his hands slid beneath her bum to angle her in a way he must have liked, Kaitlyn suddenly felt the urge to coax him towards his finish in the same way he had done with her.

"Come on Ellis," she said in her own gruff tone. "I want you to come."

"Shit," he said desperately, giving her an almost pained look as his movements began to get less coordinated. And then he pushed his forehead against hers and let out a long, low moan as she felt him jerk inside her body, causing her to flinch slightly before she quickly straightened her expression so that he wouldn't see it.

Ellis panted heavily above her, blowing his warm breath all over her face in a way she found strangely alluring, whilst his eyes stared straight into hers.

Once he'd finally calmed down, he rolled off of her, laying on his back as he stared up at the ceiling with eyes that still seemed glazed over.

"God that was good," he said, twisting his head to look at her. "Are you okay? Did you like it?"

Kaitlyn paused for a moment, wondering if it was best for her to tell him the truth or to lie.

"Um, well, I liked that you liked it."

Ellis's face immediately fell and she wished she'd decided to lie. "Oh god. I'm sorry. You should have told me to stop. I would have pulled out and we could have tried it another time."

Kaitlyn shushed him and cupped his face in her hands. "It's okay. I wanted you to enjoy it. And the pain got better in the end."

He still didn't look reassured. "Does it hurt now?"

She shifted her legs slightly, testing herself. "It aches a bit," she told him. "But it's not too bad."

He eyed her sympathetically. "I'm sorry. It will be better next time, I promise."

She smiled. "I know." Already, she couldn't wait. She wanted to experience what she'd just watched him go through.

When he climbed out of bed to go and put the condom in the bin, Kaitlyn sat up and stretched, wincing when a jolt of pain ran up between her legs.

She was curious to see if she looked any different down there after what they had done, so she pulled the duvet back to inspect herself, but widened her eyes when she saw a few small blood stains on the sheets.

"Err, Ellis, I think something's wrong."

Chapter Fourty Three

Ellis immediately ran over, looking panicked. "What is it?"

She showed him the blood, expecting him to start freaking out as much as her, but was surprised when his shoulders relaxed instead.

"Oh, yeah, I forgot to tell you about how that would happen."

Kaitlyn frowned. "What? Is it normal?"

"Yeah. It's from your hymen being broken."

She was familiar with the word and had always heard about how an intact hymen meant you were pure, but she hadn't known *where* it was or *how* it could get broken.

"Oh," she said, feeling both relieved and stupid. "Sorry, I thought you might have damaged something up there by accident.

Ellis raised his eyebrows and gave her a teasing look. "My dick's big, but it's not *that* big."

She let out an embarrassed giggle and then quickly escaped to go to the bathroom.

When she came back, Ellis had got back under the sheets so she joined him, cuddling against his chest when he pulled her into his arms.

"How do you feel?" he asked, planting a kiss on the top of her head.

"I don't know. Weird, I suppose."

"Do you feel different?"

"Yeah, I feel...changed."

He gave her an affectionate squeeze and looked down into her eyes. "I love you Kaitlyn."

"I love you too, Ellis." She leaned up to give him a peck on the lips and then got a sudden curious thought. "What was it like the first time you had sex? Does it hurt for guys too?"

He shook his head. "No, it doesn't hurt," he laughed. "It's just very quick."

She frowned up at him. "What do you mean?"

"Well, when we've not done it before, we get a bit over excited so we can't last very long before we come. But the more we do it, the more stamina we get."

"Oh." She thought about asking him just how many times he had done it, but then decided it was better for her to not know. Instead she asked, "Who was your first time with?"

He sighed, staring past her as if he was remembering. "It was a random girl I met at a party," he told her. "We'd only been in America for a few weeks at that point and everyone had been teasing me about being a virgin and how they thought I'd be waiting for marriage because I'm from England, so I just kind of did it with the first girl I met to prove a point and get them to shut up."

Kaitlyn was surprised by the information. "So, it wasn't special?"

He shook his head. "No, it's never really been special. Until now."

She smiled as she felt her whole body warm. "I'm glad there's never been anyone special for you before," she told him.

He gave her a teasing grin. "Would you have been jealous if there had been?"

"Shut up." She rolled her eyes, avoiding the question, and then let out a loud, involuntary yawn.

"Are you tired? Did I wear you out?"

"Shut up!" she told him again, hiding her face in his neck so that he wouldn't see her red cheeks.

"Sorry," he said, still laughing. His hand came up to start stroking her hair. "Just rest your eyes for ten minutes and then we'll get up."

"Okay. Don't let me go to sleep though."

"I won't."

Chapter Fourty Four

When Kaitlyn next opened her eyes, she knew immediately from the brightness of the room that it was morning.

"Oh no."

Sitting up in bed, she saw Ellis flat out beside her and she quickly shook his shoulder in an effort to wake him up.

"Ellis, we fell asleep."

It took a few moments for him to wake up and he blinked groggily, squinting against the light.

"What's wrong?"

"We fell asleep!"

She watched her words sink in and panic soon flared in his eyes. "Shit."

They both quickly jumped out of the bed, pulling their clothes back on from where they were still scattered around the floor, before they rushed out of his bedroom and down the stairs without even thinking about who else might be awake.

"Oh!" they heard Angela say in surprise as she came out of the living room, stopping them in their tracks. She looked between the pair of them curiously. "I didn't realise Kaitlyn had stayed over."

"What?!" Nicholas's voice sounded from the kitchen and he came rushing into the hallway with a broad grin on his face. "Well, well, well, from the state of you both, I'm guessing this wasn't a planned sleepover."

Ellis glared at his brother. "Of course it wasn't." He pulled Kaitlyn into his side. "Don't embarrass her."

Nicholas held up his hands defensively. "I'm not." But he was still smiling.

"I'm gonna walk Kaitlyn home," Ellis told his mum. "I'll be back in a bit."

"Okay." She eyed them warily. "Good luck."

The words twisted Kaitlyn's stomach but she forced a smile and quickly said goodbye, desperate to get away from the awkward situation even though she knew she would probably be walking into an even worse one when she got home.

Ellis guided her outside and they walked at a fast pace down the surrounding streets and through the town centre.

Once they were only a couple of minutes away from her house, Ellis stopped her and took hold of her shoulders.

"What are you gonna say when you get there?"

"I don't know!" At that moment she could only focus on not having a meltdown in public. "Do you think it's too soon to tell my mum about us? Should we just show up together so she figures out where I've been?"

Ellis gazed at her thoughtfully before taking a look around at all the people near them, some of whom were already casting inquisitive glances their way.

"What are you thinking?" she asked him.

He met her eyes, raising one eyebrow. "I've got a new plan."

And then his mouth was suddenly on hers and he was kissing her passionately, causing everything around them to go silent as a couple of dozen people stopped what they were doing to watch the spectacle happening in front of them.

Chapter Fourty Five

Kaitlyn moaned against Ellis's mouth, understanding immediately what he was doing, and wanting to put on as much of a show as possible.

The fact that she was slowly starting to find him irresistible didn't help matters.

In the end, he had to pull away first, loosening her arms from where they were gripping his t-shirt tightly, and smirking down at her. "I think your mum will probably find out on her own now."

Kaitlyn let out a giddy laugh, half terrified about what might happen now that they'd outed themselves, but also feeling strangely excited about finally having a showdown with her mum, after all the years of wanting to but having to hold her tongue in order to keep the peace.

As she scanned her gaze around all the people that had stopped to stare, she saw a few of them holding phones to their ears, talking urgently to whoever was on the other end of their calls.

"I wouldn't be surprised if she's already found out," Kaitlyn said. "Someone will have probably called her the second they saw you with me."

Ellis pulled a face. "Are you ready to go and face her?"

She nodded, telling herself to not be afraid.

He took her hand and began to pull her in the direction of her house but she quickly stopped him. "I don't think you should go with me."

He stared at her as if she was crazy. "Why not? I'm not gonna let you go alone! She might hit you or something."

Kaitlyn wasn't convinced that Ellis's presence would be enough to stop her mum from slapping her if she wanted to, but she didn't bother telling him that.

"I'll be fine," she said instead. "It's you I'd be worried about if you were there in front of her. Believe me, I'm best going alone."

He still didn't look sure. "But what if she locks you away or something? What if she tries to turn you against me?"

She laughed. "She wouldn't be able to even if she tried. I love you. She's not gonna change my mind about that."

After examining her carefully for a few more seconds, Ellis finally relented with a sigh. "Fine. You can go on your own. But call me as soon as you've finished speaking to her."

"You mean arguing with her?" Kaitlyn joked, causing him to crack a smile.

She hugged him goodbye and then walked off, straightening her back and doing her best to look confident as she rounded the corner.

But her brave facade soon slipped away when she saw both her parents glaring at her from their front window; waiting for her to get home.

Chapter Fourty Six

Kaitlyn didn't even need to get her key out because the front door was ripped open the second she stepped foot on the driveway.

"Get in here!" her mum ordered through gritted teeth, looking as though she was barely restraining herself.

Kaitlyn walked past her into the house, coming face to face with her dad who was standing in the living room with his arms folded sternly.

"What's wrong?" she asked them, feigning innocence.

Her mum just scoffed. "You know exactly what's wrong! You've been hanging around with Ellis again."

Kaitlyn shrugged. "So?"

"So, what have you been doing with him? Why were you kissing him?"

"We're together now," Kaitlyn told her calmly, trying her best to seem like she didn't see what the issue was.

Her mum immediately shook her head. "No you're not. You can't be. I forbid it."

"Well, I *am*."

"Kaitlyn!" her dad suddenly shouted. "Stop with the attitude. Listen to your mother. We don't want you with that boy. You know what people think of him and his family around here. How could you do this to us?"

She stared at him in disbelief. "I didn't do anything to you. It's no one else's business but mine and his. We love each other and we're going to be together no matter what people think." Then she decided to announce, "I'm going back to America with him."

"No you're not!" her parents shouted in unison.

"Don't be so stupid," her dad told her. "What would *you* do in America?"

"Have a normal life for once."

Her mum tutted. "A life of sin, you mean? Whatever he's told you, don't listen to it. He might have made it sound shiny and exciting but you'd hate it once you got there." Before Kaitlyn could argue back, her mum smirked. "And you've got no way to get there, anyway. You'd need a passport and one of *us* would need to sign the application for you."

Kaitlyn stared at her mum, seeing the satisfaction in her eyes because she obviously thought she'd surprised her with that bit of information.

"Are you saying you wouldn't sign it for me?"

Her mum scoffed. "Of course not. We're not letting you go anywhere."

"Even after everyone has just seen me and Ellis kissing?"

Melinda's face tightened at the reminder. "I can tell them all he kissed you against your will. They'll believe it about a guy like him."

Kaitlyn licked her lips nervously, preparing herself to drop her bombshell.

"What if I told you I'd had sex with him?" she asked, not letting herself blink or look away. "Would you be ashamed of me? Would you sign it then?"

Chapter Fourty Seven

Kaitlyn had never seen her mother look so terrifying, or her father look so disgusted.

"Tell me you're joking," her mum seethed. "Tell me you've not been stupid enough to let that boy ruin you."

Kaitlyn stared her directly in the eye. "No. I can't tell you that."

"You slut!"

Her mum suddenly lunged at her, but thankfully her father got in the way and stopped her from attacking.

"Calm down Melinda!"

Her mum twisted in his arms, trying to get away, but eventually gave up and instead just gave Kaitlyn as dark a look as she could muster.

"What have you done?" she asked her daughter. "Do you realise what this means now? Do you know what people are going to think of you?"

"I don't care," Kaitlyn said, standing her ground. "It won't matter if I move away."

Her mum just sneered. "You're not leaving! Did you really think that I'd just let you go once I knew what you'd done?"

Yes, Kaitlyn thought to herself. It was what she had counted on.

Her mum laughed at whatever expression was on her face. "Well your plan didn't work. You gave yourself to him for nothing!"

"I gave myself to him because I love him!" Kaitlyn shouted, growing more annoyed now that she couldn't figure out how the whole situation was going to end.

Her mum didn't pay any attention to her words, and instead just shook her head and told her, "I'm going to fix this."

Kaitlyn watched warily as she saw a plan start to form behind her mother's eyes.

"What do you mean?"

"I'm going to get your reputation back," Melinda told her. "I'm going to find you a husband."

Chapter Fourty Eight

"What?" Kaitlyn stared at her mum in shock. "You can't do that!"

Her mum just laughed. "Oh, believe me. I can."

"But you just said yourself that I'm ruined now," Kaitlyn reminded her desperately. "No man would want to marry me."

"I'll find one that does," her mum said confidently, as if there wasn't a doubt in her mind that she would be able to.

Before Kaitlyn could protest any further, her mum quickly spun and marched out of their front door, looking like a woman on a mission.

Kaitlyn made to go after her but her dad suddenly grabbed her arm, squeezing tightly to the point where she cried out in pain.

"You're not going anywhere Kaitlyn," he told her. "I'm not letting you near that boy again after what he's done to you."

She wanted to tell him to stop referring to Ellis as a boy when he was really a twenty eight year old *man*, but she knew it probably wasn't worth it.

She had bigger issues to worry about at that moment.

Fleeing to her room, she briefly considered climbing out of the window to sneak out again, but she knew there was a higher risk of her getting caught in daylight, especially when her dad was downstairs in front of the living room window, so she decided any kind of escape would have to wait until later in the day.

But she knew she couldn't wait that long to speak to Ellis.

Pulling out her phone, she called his number and then crouched down in the far corner of her room so that her dad would be unlikely to hear her from downstairs.

"Kaitlyn?" Ellis answered after only one ring. He sounded panicked. "What happened? What did they say?"

"Err.." She slowly told him the story of what happened from the minute her mum had opened the door, leading all the way to the aftermath of her announcing that Ellis had taken her virginity.

"So how did it get left?" Ellis asked. "Did they agree to sign the passport application?"

Kaitlyn braced herself to tell him the worst bit of news. "No, actually, mum said she's going to find me a husband and then she stormed out of the house."

There were a few seconds of shocked silence before Ellis finally managed to find his voice again.

"What?! Was she being serious? Or do you think she just said it in the heat of the moment?"

Kaitlyn remembered the vicious expression on her mum's face before she had left. "She was deadly serious."

"Shit," Ellis said, sighing heavily. "Well, don't worry. She can't make you do anything you don't want to do."

Kaitlyn interrupted him with a sarcastic scoff. "Can't she? You know how manipulative she can be."

"It doesn't matter," he said forcefully. "I'm not gonna let her control you anymore. We'll figure a way out of this. She'll have to calm down eventually, and if you make it clear to her that you're not going to give in this time, then surely she'll let you do what you want, even if she's not necessarily happy about it."

"Do you think so?" Kaitlyn asked quietly, wanting to believe what he was telling her.

"Yeah!" he said emphatically. "And besides, she's not gonna be able to find someone to marry you off to straight away, so she can't try and force you up the aisle too soon. We've still got time to try and make her see sense before things even get that far."

Chapter Fourty Nine

"Wake up!"

Kaitlyn practically jumped out of her bed when she heard her mum's screeching voice shouting in her ear.

"What's wrong?" she asked, looking between both her parents who were standing on either side of her bed, looking down on her imposingly.

Kaitlyn had decided to stay at her house the night before instead of sneaking out to see Ellis like she'd originally planned. He'd been disappointed when she'd told him, but she'd reassured him that she was only staying at her house in an effort to try and appease her parents, and not because she didn't want to see him or that she'd decided he was 'too much hassle' like he'd suggested.

"Come downstairs," her mum ordered her, leaving no room for argument.

"Why? What's going on?"

"There's someone here to see you."

Kaitlyn's stomach dropped and she immediately wanted to be sick. "Who?"

Her mum just raised a condescending eyebrow. "Come downstairs and find out."

Kaitlyn didn't think she'd ever heard such ominous words before.

Her mum fussed around her while she quickly got changed out of her pyjamas and into some normal clothes, meaning that she didn't have a chance to call Ellis before she was led downstairs to meet whoever was waiting for her.

Kaitlyn hid behind her mum, keeping her eyes trained on her feet the whole way down until they were finally in the living room and she couldn't avoid whatever was about to happen any longer.

Taking a deep breath to steady herself, she looked up and found Michael, the guy who'd got in a fight with Nicholas outside of church, standing in the centre of the room.

Kaitlyn stared at him in shock and confusion. "Um, hi."

He'd been the last person she'd expected to see, and she *really* hoped he wasn't there for the reason she thought.

But her mum soon confirmed her worst fears were right.

"Kaitlyn, you remember Michael," Melinda said, wearing an overly cheerful smile on her face. "Good news. He's agreed to marry you."

Chapter Fifty

Michael smiled at her in a way she guessed was supposed to be charming, but Kaitlyn just turned away from him and fixed a hard stare on her mother.

"Please tell me this is a joke," she said, although she knew there was no chance of that. "You seriously just went out and asked the first guy you came across if he would be willing to marry me?"

Her mum rolled her eyes as if she was being overdramatic. "Of course not. Michael's mum and I have been planning this for years, but we were planning to wait until you were both thirty before we said anything. However, because of your recent behaviour, we've had to bring the plan forward."

Kaitlyn crossed her arms. "So you were lying when you told me I could choose someone for myself?"

"No, I would have been happy to let you choose for yourself if you had wanted someone *suitable*."

She scowled at her mum. "He *is* suitable."

"No he's *not*."

Kaitlyn noticed Michael watching them, flicking his eyes from side to side with an amused expression on his face.

She blushed when she realised she probably shouldn't be discussing such matters in front of him, but the lack of surprise on his face made her guess that he already knew exactly what they were talking about anyway.

"Don't worry," he told her with a wink. "Your mum's told me about your little indiscretion. But I'm willing to forgive it." His eyes suddenly turned dark and he stared at her with a clear look of warning in his gaze as he added, "Just make sure it doesn't happen again."

Kaitlyn was so taken aback by the drastic change in his mood that she found herself unable to form words; but of course her mum was there to answer for her.

"She won't," she promised him. "I'll make sure of it. Even if I have to lock her up until the wedding day."

Michael smiled, abruptly going back to his charming persona. "Good. Thank you Melinda. I can't wait to have you as a mother in law." He settled his eyes on Kaitlyn who was still standing in a state of shell shock. "And I can't wait to have *you* as my wife."

Kaitlyn managed to choke out a sentence. "Don't I get a say in this?"

When she saw Michael's face harden, she knew she should have kept her mouth shut; and when he exchanged a knowing look with her mother, as if they'd cooked up some kind of plan together, a terrifying sense of foreboding twisted her gut.

"No, you don't get a choice," he mum told her sternly. "You're getting married in two weeks. End of story."

Chapter Fifty One

Kaitlyn spent the rest of that week locked away in her house, constantly being watched by either her mum, dad or Michael to make sure that she didn't sneak off.

They treated her like a prisoner and had taken her phone off her so that she had no way of contacting Ellis.

She knew the news of her upcoming 'wedding' had been spread around the town by her mum, so she guessed him and his family must have heard about it, but she had no way of knowing what he thought or what he was planning to do about it.

If he was planning to do something about it.

She'd hoped he might come storming round to her house, banging on the door and demanding her parents to let her out so they could be together; but that hadn't happened.

The first time she was allowed out again was to go to church the following Sunday, and she looked forward to the service more than she ever had before; both because it was a chance for her to get some fresh air, but mostly because she knew she would see Ellis.

When she and her parents arrived, Micheal and his mum and dad met them outside the church, exchanging hugs and kisses on the cheek before they all went inside to find a pew.

Kaitlyn covertly searched all the other seats for Ellis, finally breathing a sigh of relief when his gaze locked on hers from where he was sat in the back row.

She tried to give him a desperate look, almost pleading for him to do something to help, but all he did was eye the group she was with scathingly, particularly Michael, before he turned back to her and shook his head slightly.

Kaitlyn didn't understand whether he was telling her he wasn't going to do anything right then, or if he was saying he never would because he was done with her. She panicked at the thought that it might be the second option, but quickly reassured herself when she remembered him saying he loved her, and what they had shared together in his bed.

The service began then and she barely listened to a word of it; too focused on Michael's hand which seemed to purposely be resting close to her thigh.

He made her skin crawl.

Thankfully, he hadn't attempted to kiss her yet, but he had made several references to it, and had even spoken to her about how he looked forward to doing *other things* once they were married.

She promised herself she wouldn't let things get that far.

She wasn't sure how she was going to stop it, but she *would*.

Once the service was over, the congregation emptied out of the church and Kaitlyn and her group were suddenly accosted by about a dozen people who all wanted to congratulate her and Michael on their engagement.

Kaitlyn stayed quiet whilst everybody else talked, wondering what would happen if she suddenly blurted to them all that she didn't actually want to get married.

She itched to do it, but some distant sense of self preservation wouldn't let the words leave her lips.

Michael played up to the crowd, throwing his arm over her shoulder and gazing down at her like a man in love as he told them all about how happy and excited he was.

She felt sick at the sight of his act.

When the crowd eventually dispersed, breaking off into smaller groups to gossip amongst themselves, only one person was left standing there, waiting to address the 'happy couple'.

"Can I talk to you?" Ellis asked, staring directly into Michael's eyes with a challenging look in his.

Chapter Fifty Two

"No," Michael said abruptly, drawing Kaitlyn even closer into his side in what was obviously meant to be a possessive gesture.

Ellis watched the move with narrowed eyes before taking an intimidating step forward. "Get off her," he warned in a low voice. "She's *mine*."

Michael only snorted. "Not anymore, she isn't. She's going to be my wife."

Kaitlyn watched Ellis's hands clench into fists as he struggled to keep his composure.

"She's not marrying you," he said. "You can't bully her into doing it." He cast a scathing glance towards her parents who were both watching the confrontation with wide eyes. "None of you can."

Surprisingly, her dad was the first of her parents to speak for once. "Who do you think you're talking to? Get away from us. This has nothing to do with you."

Ellis gave him a disbelieving look. "I *love* her," he said passionately. "And she loves me. How the fuck can you say this has nothing to do with me?"

"Ellis." Angela's timid voice suddenly sounded from where she'd walked up behind him, and she looked nervously around the group in front of her, meeting Kaitlyn's eyes last and giving her a sad smile. "What's going on?"

"Your son's harassing us!" Kaitlyn's mum told her loudly, drawing the attention of a few people who were still standing near them.

"No I'm not," Ellis said calmly before finally meeting Kaitlyn's gaze. "I've just come to get my girlfriend back."

He reached out a hand to her in invitation.

Kaitlyn automatically moved forward to take it, but Michael quickly pulled her back, holding her against his chest so that she was unable to move.

"What do you think you're doing?" he hissed in her ear. "I told you to stay away from him."

"Get off me!" she shouted, desperately trying to free herself.

A foot suddenly shot across her line of vision and kicked Michael hard in the shin, making him immediately loosen his hold.

Kaitlyn quickly moved away and shared a smile with Nicholas, who had been the one to do the kicking, before she grasped hold of Ellis's hand.

"Let's go," she told him excitedly, feeling the adrenaline pumping through her body.

He grinned and then, like two animals fleeing from a trap, they sprinted away.

Chapter Fifty Three

Thankfully no one seemed to try to follow them, but Kaitlyn and Ellis didn't stop running until they were at his house and safely locked away inside.

They shared a laugh before Ellis suddenly became serious. "Are you okay?" He scanned every inch of her body, as if checking for any damage. "What happened? I tried calling you about a hundred times but your phone was always off."

"They took it off me," she told him. "And then they practically imprisoned me in the house and made sure that there was always one of them there to watch me to make sure that I didn't try to escape."

Ellis shook his head angrily. "They treat you like a child. It's not fair." He sighed and gave her a soft smile. "I missed you, Kaitlyn."

"I missed you too." Stepping closer, she wrapped her arms around his neck and covered his mouth with hers, kissing him enthusiastically for a few moments until he was moaning against her lips.

"I love you," he told her once they'd pulled apart.

"I love you too."

"I hated not knowing what was going on with you. And then when I heard the news about you both getting married in a couple of weeks, I was so angry that mum had to stop me from storming round to your house. I wanted to find Michael and kill him."

She pulled a face. "I wouldn't have stopped you. He's a creep."

Ellis's eyes narrowed at the word. "Has he tried to touch you?"

"No," she quickly reassured him, shaking her head. "But he's hinted about things like that. And he's just weird with how he can seem so nice and charming one minute, but then turn possessive and domineering the next."

Ellis contemplated that for a moment before saying, "Well, don't worry. I won't let him near you again."

Kaitlyn smiled and hugged him tightly, craving his touch and wanting to have as little space between them as possible after the few days they'd gone without seeing each other.

"Can we go upstairs?" she asked, trying to convey through her eyes exactly what she meant by that.

Ellis smirked. "We'll get to that later. But there's something I want to do first."

She frowned in confusion, but before she could ask what he meant, he abruptly pushed her back against the wall and knelt down in front of her. Her breathing grew heavy whilst she watched him slip his hands up her skirt to start pulling down her knickers; and once they were completely removed, he shoved them in the pocket of his jeans and gave her a lingering look, building the anticipation, before he suddenly leaned forward and buried his head between her thighs.

Chapter Fifty Four

Kaitlyn gasped desperately when she felt his tongue come out to lick her sensitive flesh, and she felt Ellis smile against her and let out a soft, breathy laugh, which only caused further sensations to ripple through her.

"Oh my god Ellis."

Her hands automatically moved to grasp the back of his head, holding him to her as he began to use his tongue to stroke her in the same way he had with his fingers a few days before.

When his tongue circled her entrance before probing inside, Kaitlyn let out an almost inhuman noise and she threw her head back against the wall, squeezing her eyes shut as pure pleasure consumed her.

As she finally began to calm down, she opened her eyes to see Ellis watching her with raised eyebrows. "That was quick," he noted, immediately making her cheeks heat.

"Is that bad?"

But he shook his head to reassure her. "Not at all. It's great, actually. I just wish I'd had the chance to taste you for longer."

She let out an embarrassed giggle and then straightened her skirt whilst he rose to his feet. "Well, feel free to do it any other time you like."

Ellis gave her a wicked grin. "I will do, don't worry."

Taking her hand, he led her up the stairs, but once they were in his room and he was kissing her neck, she suddenly stopped him.

"Wait a minute, do you think your mum and Nicholas will be coming home soon?"

"Who cares?" he murmured against her skin, planting another open mouthed kiss there.

"I don't want them to hear us!"

Ellis raised his head once more and gave her a look that could only be described as arousing. "If they come back, we'll just have to be quiet. But until then," he pulled her towards the bed. "Make as much noise as you want."

They began to kiss passionately before letting themselves fall onto the mattress. There was an eagerness about them that hadn't been there the last time, and they quickly undressed each other until they were both completely naked and Ellis was collecting another condom from his drawer.

"It shouldn't hurt this time," he told her as he rolled it on his hardness. "But if it does, tell me and I'll stop."

"Okay." Kaitlyn lay down, getting into position as she waited for him to enter her, and when he finally did she was relieved to find that there was no pain at all.

Only pleasure.

"Is that alright?" he asked, resting his forehead against hers so they were staring into each other's eyes as he thrust in and out of her. "Does it feel good this time?"

She nodded, wrapping her legs around him as she moved her hips slowly along with his. "Does it feel good for you?"

He started to laugh, but then cut off when a loud moan came out of his mouth. "It feels fucking incredible."

Just then, the sound of the front door opening travelled up the stairs, and they both abruptly paused as they listened to the voices of his mum and brother entering the house.

"Ellis, are you here?" Angela called up the stairs.

Kaitlyn panicked, looking at him with wide eyes as she began to try and push him off of her, but he resisted.

"No, don't stop," he told her quietly. "We can be quick."

She wanted to protest, but when he started pushing in and out of her even harder and faster than before, she gasped at the sensation and started moving with him again, desperate to see him come like she had the last time.

"Fuck," he muttered, kissing her sloppily as his movements became even harder.

Kaitlyn watched him, mesmerised, as he gradually fell apart above her, and she was surprised by how much more exciting the whole thing felt when she knew there was a risk of his mum and brother suddenly walking in on them.

Unexpectedly, she sensed the telltale sensations of her own finish, and she had to bury her head into his neck and moan as quietly as possible against his skin as her body shook.

Ellis laughed breathlessly, smiling down at her with a warm look in his eyes. "Did you come?"

She nodded and a self satisfied smirk stretched across his face before his brow furrowed and his pelvis began to hit hers with more determination, telling her that he was nearing his own end.

Kaitlyn kept her gaze locked on his, marvelling at his clenched jaw and black eyes as he struggled to not make a noise.

When he came, he buried his head against her shoulder just like she had with him, and she felt the vibrations of his silent moans on her skin before he collapsed heavily on top of her.

Chapter Fifty Five

"Ellis? Kaitlyn? Are you here?"

Angela's voice called for them again, closer than it had been before, and they quickly realised she was coming up the stairs.

"Shit. Get dressed," Ellis told her, jumping out of bed and throwing her clothes to her as he hurriedly pulled his own back on.

When Angela knocked on his bedroom door, they were both still in a state of disarray and the bed was a mess, but they were at least not naked any more.

"Yeah?" Ellis responded when his mum knocked again.

Kaitlyn was relieved when she didn't enter the room and instead stayed outside.

"I just wanted to check that you're both okay."

"Yeah, we're fine." he met Kaitlyn's eyes. "What happened at the church after we left?"

"Both sets of parents weren't very happy." They heard her sigh through the door. "And that horrible Michael wanted to come back to the house with us but I warned them that if any of them tried to follow I'd call the police."

Kaitlyn smiled and called, "Thanks Angela."

"You're welcome dear," the older woman responded, with a smile in her voice. "I know you probably want some time alone together so just both come down when you're ready."

"We will," Ellis promised, and then they listened to his mum walk back downstairs before both sinking back against his pillows.

"Do you really think they'll all stay away just because your mum threatened to involve the police?" she asked him, not really believing it herself.

Ellis sighed. "No, I don't. At least not for long. I'm surprised they didn't just follow her straight here anyway. Makes me think they might be planning something else."

It was an exhausting thought.

Kaitlyn just wanted it all to end and for her and Ellis to be left alone.

Her eyes suddenly noticed something on his leg, and she quickly sat up. "When did you do this?" she asked him, tracing her fingers over the fresh tattoo of her name that had been added to the pattern on his calf.

Ellis smiled almost self consciously. "I did it yesterday. Thought it was a good way to finish the tattoo off."

"It is." She ran her fingers over it once more, feeling flattered that he'd chosen to ink her name into his skin, where it would stay for the rest of his life.

In some ways, the gesture seemed even more powerful than when he'd told her he loved her.

Meeting his eyes, she grinned as she came to a decision.

"I want one."

Chapter Fifty Six

Ellis raised his eyebrows, giving her a sceptical look. "What do you mean you want one?"

"I want a tattoo of your name. And I want you to do it for me."

Kaitlyn had thought he'd be excited about the idea of her wanting his name permanently put on her body, but apparently not.

"You don't like needles," he reminded her. "And you're still trying to get out of an engagement your mum's forced you into. If she found out you'd got a tattoo she'd probably go crazy. Surely it would just make matters worse?"

She just smiled smugly. "Yeah, it would. That's the whole point. I doubt Michael would want to marry me when I've got another man's name marked forever on my skin."

Kaitlyn watched the understanding appear in Ellis's eyes, but he still didn't seem sure about the plan.

"I don't think you should get it done, just to get one over on your mother," he told her, causing her to roll her eyes.

It was like the argument they'd had about her losing her virginity all over again.

"I'm not only doing it for that," she said. "It's just an added bonus, but really what I care about the most is having your name on me in the same way you now have mine on you."

She stroked his tattoo again as he finally relaxed. "Okay, if you're really sure about this, then I'll do it."

"Great." She smiled. "Let's do it now."

He laughed. "Seriously? Don't you think you should think about it for a bit longer?"

But she was adamant. "No. I want it now. Before my mum comes looking for me and can lock me away from you again."

The reminder of the situation they still had hanging over their heads gave him a new sense of urgency, and he quickly agreed before going over to his draws to collect his kit.

As he laid it out on the bed, Kaitlyn examined the needles and different coloured inks curiously, feeling a nervousness start in her stomach.

"Where do you want it?" Ellis asked her.

She thought for a moment and then grinned, lifting up her top and pointing towards the bit of her left breast that spilled out over her bra.

"Here."

Chapter Fifty Seven

Ellis got his equipment ready, slipping a black latex glove on his hand and wiping the area the tattoo would be going on before meeting her eyes with a smirk on his face.

"I can't believe you're actually doing this," he said. "Last chance to back out."

Kaitlyn shook her head. "Nope. Do it."

The sound of the needle suddenly vibrating shocked her and she stared at it warily as he brought it towards the skin of her breast.

Her whole body tensed up, waiting for it to touch her, and when it did she couldn't decide whether she liked the sensation or not. It wasn't painful necessarily, but it did sting slightly and it was just....weird.

"Are you okay?" Ellis asked, not looking away from what he was doing as he moved the needle slowly across her skin.

"Yeah, I'm fine."

Her hands were gripping the bed sheets tightly and she couldn't relax whilst he was doing it, even though she'd now found out it wasn't too bad. She still didn't trust that it wouldn't suddenly start hurting and so she held her breath the entire time.

"Done," Ellis said about twenty minutes later, pulling the needle away and examining his work.

Kaitlyn opened her eyes and looked down at what he'd done, seeing his name written in swirling black ink right above her bra line.

The skin around it was red, and she stayed silent as Ellis put some kind of cream over the tattoo before surprisingly wrapping cling film around her chest.

"You'll need to keep this on for a few hours just to protect it," he explained. "What do you think?"

She stared at it in fascination, unable to grasp the concept that it would still be there in decades to come.

"I love it."

Chapter Fifty Eight

The two of them went downstairs a short while later, joining Angela and Nicholas in the living room.

"Finished having sex now?" Nicholas asked his brother, giving them both a cheeky wink.

Ellis grabbed a cushion from the couch and threw it at him.

"Are you okay, honey?" Angela asked Kaitlyn as they sat down. "I've been worried about you these last few days."

"I'm alright. Now that I've got away from them all, anyway."

"That Michael guy is a dick," Nicholas suddenly broke in to say. "If your mum was so insistent on finding you a husband, she could have at least looked for a nicer guy for you."

Kaitlyn laughed. "Apparently she'd been planning it with his parents for years."

"What?" Ellis was shocked. She hadn't had a chance to tell him the full story yet.

"Yeah, she told me she'd basically always had him ready as a backup option in case I didn't choose anyone 'suitable' myself."

Ellis scoffed. "Did *he* know that this whole time as well?"

"I'm not sure. I never asked him. All he told me was that my mum had told him the full story about what had happened with you, and he was willing to forgive my 'indiscretion' as he put it."

Ellis seemed to be getting angrier by the second and she decided it was probably best to not tell him anymore. She didn't want him to go looking for Michael to have some kind of showdown with him. It would just make everything worse.

"That guy's gonna get what's coming to him," he said darkly, causing Angela and Kaitlyn to exchange a nervous look.

"Well," Nicholas said. "You're gonna have to sort out this mess soon, because we're due to be going home in two weeks, and if Kaitlyn wants a passport, she's gonna have to send the application like *tomorrow*."

"What?" Kaitlyn started panicking. "Have you already booked your flights? I thought you were staying longer?"

Angela gave her a sympathetic look. "Well, we reckon we'll be finished with the house by then, and we're not exactly welcome around here so we decided to leave sooner."

"Don't worry," Ellis said, taking hold of her hand. "I've already told you I won't be leaving with them unless you're coming too. I can just stay longer if necessary."

"Err, Ellis, what about your job?" his brother reminded him, but Ellis just shot him a quick look to tell him to be quiet.

Kaitlyn looked between the three of them wildly, scared that they would all leave her alone in England to deal with the mess she'd made. She knew Ellis couldn't stay with her forever because he had a life in America to get back to; and she knew she had a new life to *start* over there, so didn't want to delay it for much longer and risk having the whole plan fall apart.

"I need to sort this out once for all," she decided, speaking out loud. "I need to confront my mum and Michael. And I need to do it *now*."

Chapter Fifty Nine

Kaitlyn stood up before anyone had even had a chance to respond. "I'm going to go and talk to them," she announced to the room before swiftly turning around and marching purposely towards the front door.

"Kaitlyn, wait." Ellis chased after her, catching hold of her arm. "You don't have to rush into this just because you're worried about us leaving. How about you take a night to figure out what you want to say to them, and then we can both go and see them tomorrow?"

Kaitlyn considered his words, wondering if he was right or if it would be better for her to strike quickly whilst her anger was still at the surface.

Coming to a decision, she opened her mouth to tell him that she didn't want to wait, but was suddenly interrupted by five loud bangs on the door.

"Kaitlyn!" her mum's voice shouted through the wood. "Enough of this! We've given you enough time to see sense on your own. Open the door and come home with us."

Ellis and Kaitlyn exchanged a startled look as Angela and Nicholas came running out of the living room to see what was going on.

Her mum banged again.

"Stop behaving like a child. You're too old for this. Get out here now, while your fiancé is still willing to forgive you."

Kaitlyn's hands curled into fists as she felt herself getting more and more wound up by her mother's words.

The final straw came when she recognised the sound of Michael's voice discussing something with her parents outside, and she flew into action, ripping open the door and staring at the three of them with the most threatening look she could muster.

"Leave me alone," she told them, enunciating the words clearly so that they'd understand how serious she was. "I'm not marrying Michael, and I'm not coming home with you. I'm staying here."

Her mum completely ignored her words and instead pushed past her into the house, with her dad and Michael following closely behind.

The seven of them formed a sort of circle in the entryway, all eyeing each other warily and waiting for someone to make the next move.

Surprisingly, it was Angela who spoke first.

"Melinda," she said wearily, addressing her old friend. "Just let your daughter do what she wants. If you try and force her down the aisle, you could ruin your relationship with her forever."

"I don't care," her mum spat. "It's better than having her reputation ruined which it would be if people found out she'd chosen to join a family like yours."

Kaitlyn rolled her eyes to herself. "Mum, shut up! I don't care about my reputation or yours. I only care about being happy and being with someone that I love. And that's not *him*."

Michael only seemed amused by her words, as if he thought the way she was behaving was cute. It made her hate him even more.

Storming into the living room for a moment, she came back out with the passport application clutched in her hands.

"I'm going to America, mum." She held the form out to her, willing her to take it as she spoke through gritted teeth. "So sign the *fucking* application."

A white hot rage appeared in her mum's eyes for a moment, and Kaitlyn worried that she might actually attack her, but it disappeared as quickly as it had come and her mum put on a calm facade as she smirked at her daughter cruelly.

"No. I'm never signing that form, so you're never leaving the country. That's all there is to it."

Kaitlyn glared at her, seeing the self-satisfaction in her expression because she thought she'd won and that Kaitlyn would have no choice but to give in and do what she said.

But Kaitlyn still had one card to play.

"Will this change your mind?" she asked, staring her mum directly in the eyes as she abruptly yanked down the neckline of her top, exposing her chest and the cling film wrapped tattoo that was now permanently a part of her.

Chapter Sixty

Melinda stared in horror at Kaitlyn's chest while her dad and Angela gasped in shock. Nicholas found it funny and struggled to contain his laughter when he saw his brother's name emblazoned across her breast, but a hard nudge to the side from Ellis quickly shut him up.

Kaitlyn didn't bother looking at Michael to see his reaction, because she didn't care about it or him.

All of her focus was on her mother who seemed to have gone pale, and who was blinking rapidly as if she thought the tattoo might disappear if she did it enough times.

As Ellis came to stand beside Kaitlyn protectively, her mum turned her hate filled stare on him. "Did *you* do this to her?"

"She asked me to. It was her idea."

"You fucking prick!"

At once, everyone turned to look at Michael who had suddenly decided to speak up.

When he locked eyes with Kaitlyn, she flinched, having never seen somebody so angry before, and she took an automatic step back.

"What the fuck have you done?" he roared. "I'm not marrying you now, you little bitch."

"No," her mum gasped, reaching out for him, but he shook her off.

"No, Melinda. Forgiving her lack of virginity was one thing, but I'm not marrying her when she has another man's name basically engraved into her skin."

Kaitlyn couldn't help but smirk as she watched their interaction, knowing her plan had been successful for once.

"What the fuck are you smiling at?" Michael asked once he noticed her amusement. "Don't laugh at me you stupid whore."

His hand suddenly swung up and struck her across the face, making her lose her balance from the shock of it.

Immediately, Ellis stepped in, grabbing hold of the front of Michael's shirt and pushing his face close to his.

"Don't fucking touch her," he warned menacingly. "If it wasn't for the fact that I know you'd get me arrested for assault, I'd beat the shit out of you and prove that you're not as tough as you like to think you are. But instead I'm just gonna warn you to stay the fuck away from her and never let me see you again."

Kaitlyn watched Michael's throat move as he swallowed nervously. His usually confident persona was gone and, in that moment, he just looked like a scared bully who wasn't used to having people stand up to him.

"Okay fine," he said, in a voice that was clearly trying to sound brave. "Get off me and I'll go. I don't want any part in this shit anymore."

Ellis gave him a final warning look and then pushed him away, keeping his eyes on him until he'd disappeared out the door and set off jogging down the street.

The remaining members of the group turned to face each other.

Melinda seemed devastated, and looked like she was struggling to understand how her plan could have crumbled in only a matter of minutes.

Her dad was wearing a blank expression, but he had rested a hand on her mum's shoulder in an obvious gesture to show that whatever her mum did next, he would be on her side.

But Kaitlyn no longer cared about them, their anger, or their self pity.

Silently, she raised the passport application again and held it out to her mother who then eyed it warily, still not reaching to take it.

"If you don't sign it," Kaitlyn told her in a soft voice. "I'll show everyone in town my tattoo, and I'll make sure that your reputation is ruined just as much as mine."

Melinda scowled at her, looking as though she wanted to argue, but a warning squeeze of the shoulder from her husband made her finally sigh in defeat.

With a trembling hand, she reached for the form.

Chapter Sixty One

Kaitlyn's parents left before the ink had even dried on the paper.

Her mum clearly wasn't happy with how things had turned out but she'd obviously realised that she'd never be able to find another man to marry her daughter off to when Kaitlyn had a tattoo of Ellis's name on her chest.

"Do you think she'll burn all my stuff before I have a chance to go and collect it?" Kaitlyn joked to the others.

Ellis wrapped his arm around her and placed a light kiss on her mouth. "Don't worry about them. Just think about yourself from now on and the new life we're going to have together."

She couldn't help but feel giddy at the reminder, and it was almost hard for her to believe that it was actually happening.

She was going to America.

The next ten days or so were surreal.

Kaitlyn stayed with Ellis and his family at their house and helped them to finish clearing everything out so that the house could be put up for sale and they could all leave.

Their plane tickets were bought and Kaitlyn's visa and passport were sorted out, meaning that the only thing left to do was pack.

But that wasn't so easy in Kaitlyn's case.

She hadn't been back to her parent's house since the day her mum had finally signed the form, and she hadn't even received a text or phone call to check that she was alright.

So far, she'd just been wearing Angela's clothes to save her from having any more confrontations with her mum and dad; but as their leaving date got nearer, she knew it was time for her to go home and face them so that she could pack up her stuff.

She really wasn't looking forward to it.

"I'll go with you," Ellis told her as she was getting ready to go. "Maybe it will be easier if I'm there."

She gave him a sceptical look. "No offence, but I just think you'd make things worse and they'd be even more antagonistic."

He finally relented and she set off across town to make her way 'home', noticing a lot of nasty looks being passed her way, but she purposely ignored them and didn't let them bother her.

She didn't know what story her mum would have told people to explain why her daughter was suddenly leaving to go and live in another country with a family they all disliked, but she decided it was probably better for her not to find out.

Her mum wouldn't be able to affect her for much longer.

When she arrived at the house she was annoyed, but not really surprised, to find that they'd changed the locks. Rolling her eyes, Kaitlyn knocked on the door and waited anxiously until her dad finally opened it.

She forced a smile. "Hi dad."

"What do you want?"

"Oh, err, I've come to pack up my stuff."

He stared at her blankly, not showing any reaction to her words, and then just stepped back to let her inside.

Her mum appeared from the kitchen. "What do you want?"

Kaitlyn sighed. "I've come to pack up my stuff. We're leaving for America in a couple of days."

Melinda's back straightened. "You're really going?"

"Of course. I told you I was."

Surprisingly, her mum's eyes teared up. "So you want nothing to do with us anymore?"

"I didn't say that. I can still call you, or you could come and visit."

Her mum scoffed. "I'm not going over *there*."

"Well, that's your choice. But, either way, I'm leaving."

Kaitlyn headed straight upstairs, not wanting to argue with her mother anymore than they already had, and not wanting to get wrapped up in any more drama.

Her room was exactly as she'd left it, and she quickly went round and piled everything up that she wanted to take with her. The rest she would leave for her parents to deal with.

She'd never been on holiday so didn't have a suitcase to pack everything up in. Ellis had bought her one to take to America with her, but for the moment she was just using a roll of bin bags that Angela had given her.

All in all, it took her about an hour and a half to sort everything out.

Her parents didn't disturb her during that time, but when she went back downstairs with her collection of bin bags, their conversation abruptly stopped so she guessed that they had been discussing her.

"Um, well, I'm done," she told them awkwardly. "Everything else you can just throw away if you want."

Her mum nodded once. "Okay."

"So...I'm gonna go."

Kaitlyn waited for them to wish her luck or at least hug her goodbye, but when they just stayed where they were, expressionless, she started to make her way towards the door.

"You could have at least offered me a lift," she muttered under her breath as she struggled to balance the weight of the bags in her arms.

Just as she'd managed to navigate her way out the door and was about to close it behind her, her mum finally decided to speak up.

"Kaitlyn."

She turned to her mum, feeling hopeful that she might want to leave things on a good note between them, but as Melinda walked towards her with her familiar piercing glare, Kaitlyn knew immediately that wouldn't be the case.

"I'm ashamed of you," her mum told her. "You'll regret this one day and realise you made a mistake, but don't you dare think you can come back here. I want nothing to do with you from this day onwards."

Kaitlyn stared at her mother in shock, unable to fathom why she'd choose to be so nasty when she could potentially be seeing her only daughter for the last time.

Looking at her dad, who seemed to be cowering behind Melinda, she waited for him to finally speak up against his wife and defend his daughter; but of course that didn't happen.

He just avoided her gaze and kept his eyes trained on the wall so he wouldn't have to acknowledge what had just been said.

Shaking her head in disbelief, Kaitlyn said sarcastically, "No problem. Thanks for the heartfelt goodbye."

She marched off down the street, dragging her bags at her side, and was aware of about a dozen sets of eyes all peaking around her neighbour's curtains to watch her go.

Chapter Sixty Two

"I'm too excited to go to sleep," Kaitlyn told Ellis, like a giddy child who was wide awake on Christmas Eve.

They were all getting up early the next morning to go to the airport, and then Kaitlyn would be going on a plane for the first time ever in her life, and leaving the only country and way of life she'd ever known.

It was nerve wracking and thrilling all at the same time.

Ellis laughed at what she'd said. "You're so cute. I don't think you've stopped smiling all day."

Her cheeks heated but she knew he wouldn't be able to tell through the darkness in his bedroom.

"Are you excited to be going home?" she asked him, suddenly realising that with everything that had been going on with her, she'd never actually spoken to him about it.

"Yeah," he said immediately. "I can't wait. But I did end up having a better time here than I'd originally planned, so at least I've got some good memories to take with me."

Kaitlyn grinned. "Memories with me?"

"Of course."

"Do you think we'll ever come back to England one day?"

He sighed, taking a moment to consider the question. "Maybe. I'd like to think that it will move with the times eventually and start living like the rest of the world, but I doubt that's gonna happen any time soon."

He stroked her hair back from her forehead and then asked in a low voice, "Will you miss it here?"

Kaitlyn shrugged. "Parts of it, I suppose. I'm not really sure how much though. I guess I'll just find out once I get to America and have to start making a life there."

"Do you think there's a chance you could change your mind and want to come back like your mum said?"

"Definitely not."

She leaned up to kiss him, meaning for it to be brief, but ending up with his tongue in her mouth as she pulled him on top of her body.

"Are you still not tired?" he murmured against her lips.

She shook her head and then kissed him more eagerly as she felt his hand start to slide beneath her pyjama shorts.

Chapter Sixty Three

Airports were terrifying.

At least, that's what Kaitlyn thought by the time she'd been through the check in process and security.

There were so many *people*. She'd had to grip Ellis's hand tightly the whole time because she was so worried about losing him in the crowds.

He, on the other hand, was perfectly at ease and navigated his way around completely unbothered.

"If you think this is busy, wait until you get to New York," Nicholas told her. "It's permanent chaos there."

Kaitlyn's eyes widened in alarm but Ellis quickly reassured her that his brother was exaggerating.

As they boarded their flight a couple of hours later, she noted that, just like when they'd been checking in, there didn't seem to be many English people leaving the country, and she wondered just how rare it was for someone like her to escape and go to start a new life somewhere.

"Why would people from other countries come here on holiday?" she asked Ellis as they took their seats on the plane. "Wouldn't they find it really boring?"

He shrugged. "I think they're probably just interested to see if it's really as bad as it sounds. People talk about England a lot and how weird it is, but I think some people kind of have to see it to believe it."

"Oh." Kaitlyn thought for a moment. "So will people think I'm weird, because I'm from England? Will they make fun of me?" She remembered what he'd told her about how he'd lost his virginity to a random girl because he'd been getting teased after he'd first moved.

"No." Ellis shook his head a bit too quickly, making Kaitlyn wonder if he wasn't being completely honest. "And anyway, if anyone tries to make fun of you, I'll stop them."

She supposed it was the best reassurance she could get.

"Do you think your friends will like me?"

At that, he smiled. "Yeah, definitely. I can't wait for you to meet them, and to show you off."

Kaitlyn looked at him sceptically. "Show me off?"

"Yep. I've not told any of them about you coming home with me so I think they'll be very surprised when I introduce them to my girlfriend."

She wasn't sure that was a good thing, but she didn't comment.

The plane took off soon after and it took her well over an hour to finally relax back against her seat instead of hanging on to the headrest in front of her because she was so terrified about suddenly plummeting back down to earth.

Ellis found her fear hilarious but he gave her some headphones because he suggested that listening to music might calm her down.

Thankfully, it did; to the point where she was asleep within minutes.

The next time she opened her eyes, it was because Ellis was whispering in her ear.

"We're here, baby."

Chapter Sixty Four

It was just nearing 5pm New York time when they left the airport.

Kaitlyn was exhausted because of the time difference and the early start she'd had that morning, but she willed her body to stay alert so that she could take in every detail of her surroundings during the taxi drive to Ellis's apartment.

"I won't be far," Angela told her as she hugged Kaitlyn goodbye at the taxi rank. "My house is only about a twenty minute walk from Ellis's place so you can come and see me any time you want."

"I will," Kaitlyn said, hugging her tightly. It was sad for her to think that Angela was now the closest thing she had to a mother.

"And me and Tipp are only a few blocks away from mum," Nicholas added. "I can't wait for you to meet him."

Kaitlyn couldn't wait either.

She hadn't heard too much about Nicholas's boyfriend, but she knew from how happy he got when he spoke about him that Tipp must be a special person.

"Come on," Ellis said, guiding her into a taxi once he'd loaded their suitcases and his mum and brother had gone off in their own cabs. "Let's go home."

It was about a half an hour drive to Ellis's apartment, and Kaitlyn practically had her face glued to the window for the whole journey, staring out in fascination at the bright lights and tall skyscrapers she saw along the way.

"Wow," she said over and over again, or she would point something out to Ellis as if he wouldn't have already noticed it during the thirteen years he'd lived there.

When they arrived outside his apartment complex, Ellis paid the driver and then led her inside and up to the sixth floor.

The building was fancier than any she'd ever seen before, and a new kind of excitement started in her belly as she waited to see the place that she would be living in from that point onwards.

As soon as Ellis had opened his front door, her eyes widened and she stepped inside in an almost daze, with her eyes quickly flicking around the large space, trying to take in every feature.

"Do you like it?" Ellis asked, once he'd given her a bit of time to explore the main room.

"I love it," she said. "I can't believe you actually own this place."

He showed her the bathroom and what would be their bedroom next.

"I'll clear some space for you in the wardrobe so you can put your clothes in there," he told her. "And I've got an extra day off work tomorrow so we can go out and get you anything else you need."

"Okay. Cool."

Kaitlyn sat down on the bed, looking around in wonder as she struggled to take everything in. "I'm actually here," she said, almost to herself.

"Yeah, you are." Ellis came to sit beside her and stared deeply into her eyes. "You're free."

Chapter Sixty Five

Kaitlyn's new reality still hadn't sunk in a week later.

She'd spent the past seven days exploring the city with Ellis every chance she got, but she thought she could wander the streets for ten years and still not discover everything there was to see or do.

Whilst Ellis was at work, Kaitlyn stayed at home as she was too scared to go out alone in case she got lost and couldn't find her way back.

They had fallen into a good routine of going for a walk after dinner every night, heading in a new direction each time they did so.

Angela had come round to see her one day when she was in on her own and it had been nice to have company, especially from a motherly figure.

Unsurprisingly, her own mum hadn't tried to contact her; not even to check that she'd got there safely. Kaitlyn wouldn't put it past her mum to have actually deleted her phone number the second she knew she was no longer on English soil, but she didn't let it bother her and just focused on enjoying her new life.

She had at first been eager to look for a job as she wanted to start earning money to help pay the bills, but Ellis had reassured her that he could afford things on his own for the time being and so they had decided that she should start looking for work once she was more familiar with the area and didn't find just the thought of going outside on her own intimidating.

Ellis had stayed in with her every night that week once they'd come home from their walks, but she knew he'd received a lot of messages from his friends inviting him out to somewhere or other because they wanted to catch up with him after not seeing him for so long, so she'd urged him to go out that weekend because she didn't want to be ruining his social life.

"It's fine," he had reassured her, but she hadn't taken no for an answer.

"Okay, I'll go," he'd finally agreed. "But I want you to come with me so you can meet everyone."

Kaitlyn hadn't been so sure about that part.

She was still so *afraid* of everything, and she'd never been particularly good at meeting new people, so she was worried that the combination of both would lead to a few awkward encounters with his mates and that they might end up hating her because of it.

"They'll like you. I promise," Ellis had said sincerely, and she'd had no reason to doubt him so had eventually agreed to go.

After all, the more she put off meeting them, the more awkward it would likely be when she finally did.

As she got dressed on the following Saturday night to go to the bar they were all meeting at, she decided to put on the dress that she'd bought for the first night she'd gone round for tea at Angela's house. It was probably the nicest thing she owned and would hopefully stop her from standing out too much from the rest of the girls in the bar.

"You look lovely," Ellis said, coming up behind her and wrapping his arms around her waist as she examined herself in the mirror. "I loved this dress the first time I saw you wearing it, I was just too stubborn to mention it then."

The new piece of information made her smile as she finished off getting ready.

"So, I definitely look okay then?" she asked him one last time before they left. "This dress isn't too frumpy?"

He ran his gaze up and down her body, taking in the knee length black dress with capped sleeves. "Yeah, don't worry. It's nice. It's just....conservative. But in a sexy way."

Kaitlyn frowned, unsure how she felt about that, but then the taxi arrived and it was too late for her to change so she told herself to stop worrying.

They're Ellis's friends, she reminded herself as she climbed in the back of the cab. *They're not going to be cruel to you, no matter what you're wearing.*

Chapter Sixty Six

Kaitlyn regretted her decision to go to the bar the minute the taxi dropped them off outside and she saw the streams of people through the doors, and heard the pounding music which she knew would just get louder once they were actually inside.

"Are you okay?" Ellis asked, taking her hand.

"Yeah," she forced a smile on her face, hoping it looked genuine. "Just a bit nervous."

She didn't want to ruin his night by telling him the truth.

"I told you, it'll be fine." He squeezed her hand reassuringly and then pulled her past the bouncer and through the doors into the dimly lit bar.

They'd only been inside for a matter of seconds before they heard multiple voices shout, "Ellis!", before a group of about nine or ten people came rushing over to pat him on the back and give him warm hugs.

Kaitlyn stayed on the periphery of them all, watching as Ellis began to answer his friends' questions about what England had been like and if he'd missed them etc.

After a couple of minutes, one of the girls in the group finally noticed her standing there, and she gave her an odd look. "Who's this?"

"Oh yeah," Ellis said, as if he'd just remembered Kaitlyn's presence. He wrapped his arm around her waist and brought her closer to his side. "This is Kaitlyn. My girlfriend."

All of his friends' mouths collectively dropped open in shock before they all started speaking at once.

"Your *girlfriend*?"

"Well you kept this quiet!"

"I didn't think I'd ever see a day where you actually decided to have a relationship with someone."

Kaitlyn frowned at that comment.

"Where did you meet?" one of the guys asked, and everyone stopped talking to listen intently.

"In England," Ellis told them. "And we actually met years ago. We were best friends before I moved here."

Everyone continued to stare at her as if they'd just discovered a creature which they'd thought didn't exist.

The boys seemed more excited by the news than the females in the group who all started to give Kaitlyn dirty looks as they ran their narrowed gazes over her.

She even thought she heard one of the girls lean over to her friend to say, "What the fuck is she wearing?" before they burst out laughing, but she couldn't be sure that it wasn't her own paranoia making her imagine things.

"Wait, is she the girl you told us about when you first moved here?" one of the guys suddenly said, drawing Kaitlyn's attention to him and making her smile at the thought that Ellis might have been pining for her back then.

But any hopes of that quickly disappeared when the guy opened his mouth to speak again.

"You know, the one you used to make fun of for being really weird and *plain*, as you put it?"

Chapter Sixty Seven

Kaitlyn's stomach sank, and her eyes immediately moved to Ellis, but he seemed to be purposely avoiding her gaze as he smiled at his friend and tried to play down the situation.

"Yeah, but you know, she's cool now," was all he said, which just made Kaitlyn feel worse.

She kept her gaze on him as he continued to chat and joke with his friends, but he didn't look her way once. In fact, none of the guys did. Only the girls who were still assessing her and making it immediately clear that they wouldn't be looking to make friends with her.

Their behaviour was making Kaitlyn feel nervous, because she could only imagine one reason why Ellis's female friends would all seem to have such a problem with her, but she did her best to ignore it for the time being because she had other things to worry about, and wasn't going to question Ellis about them when they were only a few feet away.

So Kaitlyn stayed quiet, listening to the conversations around her but not taking part in any; both because nobody seemed interested in getting to know her, and because she was in a weird mood after what she'd heard about Ellis.

She followed the group to the bar when they all went to get a drink, and then again stayed on the outskirts, people watching and taking in everything that was happening around her.

She'd never been in a bar before, and had never seen drunk people, so it was strange to see how differently everyone acted compared to the composed English people she had always known.

"Do you drink?" one of Ellis's guy friends suddenly asked her when he realised she was the only one without a glass.

"Err, not alcohol," she told him, making a condescending smile appear on his face.

"I didn't think you would. How about I just get you a water?"

A few of the others in the group laughed at his words, and Kaitlyn searched Ellis out, hoping he would defend her, but saw that he was too busy talking to a couple of the girls in the group to even notice what was going on.

"No thanks," she muttered, turning away quickly to go and seek out the toilets so that she could hide for a while.

When she found them, she locked herself in a cubicle and began to cry. She knew she shouldn't have gone out with Ellis, and she cursed herself for not following her instincts.

It took about ten minutes for her to compose herself, and she reluctantly left the safety of the toilets and made her way back over to the group, stopping to hide behind a couple of people when she heard her name being mentioned.

"Is that girl really your girlfriend?" one of the blonde women was asking Ellis as the group all crowded around him.

"Yeah, what's wrong with that? Don't you like her?"

"I'm surprised you like her," one of the guys said. "She doesn't seem like your usual type."

Ellis shrugged, seeming uncomfortable with all the questions. "So?"

"So, I just think it's a bit stupid that you moved her over here from England after only spending a few weeks with her."

"But we were friends when we were kids," Ellis reminded him.

"Yeah, but you always said she was a bit of a freak," another girl said. "You always made it sound like you hated her."

Surprisingly, Ellis didn't deny that.

"Well, I'm happy," he told them. "Isn't that all that matters?"

He got a few reluctant agreements but the rest of the group just stayed quiet.

Kaitlyn chose that moment to pretend to come back from the toilet, and she sidled up beside Ellis, feeling uncomfortable around him after everything she'd heard but knowing he was the only person she was safe with there.

"You okay?" he asked her. "Do you want a drink?"

"No, I'm fine, thanks."

He gave her a small smile and put his arm around her waist before turning back to his friends and starting new conversations with them.

No one spoke to Kaitlyn for the rest of the night; her boyfriend included.

Chapter Sixty Eight

Kaitlyn was raging by the time they all left the bar; and just when she thought she could finally go home and get some peace, Ellis decided to invite all his friends back to the apartment.

She'd not spoken for hours and had only watched whilst other girls blatantly flirted with her boyfriend in front of her, and whilst the boys all made sly comments about virgins and prudes which were obviously directed at her even though they never mentioned her by name.

Ellis had only laughed at his friends, or casually turned the girls down, but he hadn't actually defended Kaitlyn or told everyone to stop treating her so badly.

To be honest, he had acted like an idiot for the entire night, and it was almost as if he'd turned into a different person from the one she'd always known the second he'd met up with his friends.

He and the group had all been taking stupid pictures of themselves and uploading them to different websites she'd never heard of before, and when they hadn't been doing that they'd been going outside every half an hour to smoke something called a vape which was apparently a way to help people stop smoking, even though she doubted any of the group had been addicted to cigarettes in the first place.

None of it made sense to her, and she felt like an alien as she watched their strange behaviour, and the pathetic jokes they made with each other, which Ellis gladly went along with while ignoring the fact she was with him altogether.

Kaitlyn didn't even get a chance to speak to him in the taxi on the way back to his apartment because a couple of the girls jumped in with them, talking loudly and singing along to the radio because they were well past drunk by that point.

An hour or so later, the same two girls were making out on the couch whilst the guys stood around to watch, exchanging smirks and rude jokes about how they wanted to join in.

"What about you Ellis?" the dark haired girl asked in a voice which could only be described as seductive. "Do you want to join in for old times' sake?"

Kaitlyn felt sick, and she quickly moved out of the room whilst she heard the guys all joking behind her.

Collapsing onto her bed, tears started to pour from her eyes again, even heavier than they had been in the toilets earlier in the night.

"What am I doing here?" she asked aloud to the empty room, suddenly wondering if, after everything, her mum might have been right and she'd made a mistake by moving there.

She'd gone to America to start a new life with Ellis, and it had been going so well, but the other side of him she'd seen whilst he'd been with his friends was someone she didn't like, and she couldn't help but question whether he had really been worth it.

Chapter Sixty Nine

Kaitlyn fell asleep at some point and then was woken a few hours later by the sound of everyone saying loud goodbyes in the living room.

"Good to see you again guys," she heard Ellis say.

"See you soon," another guy said.

"Aren't you going to give me a kiss goodnight?"

Kaitlyn scowled when she heard one of the girls say that, but her only relief was that a few seconds later all of the guys started teasing her about how she'd been rejected by Ellis.

"Maybe leave your girlfriend at home next time," one of the guys said next. "She's not exactly fun, is she?"

"Shut up," Ellis laughed. "She's not that bad."

It was the closest he'd come to sticking up for her all night, but he didn't exactly sound offended by his friend's words.

When they had all finally left, Kaitlyn listened to Ellis tidying the place up and throwing away numerous glass bottles before he went to the bathroom to seemingly get ready for bed.

He joined her in the room a few minutes later and she kept her back to him as he took his clothes off and climbed under the covers, hoping that he would assume she was asleep because she didn't want to confront him about his behaviour when it was the early hours of the morning and he was drunk.

Thankfully, he didn't try to speak to her, and instead just placed a few sloppy kisses on her cheek and breathed in the scent of her hair as he said, "I love you baby."

Then he rolled over and was snoring within seconds.

Ellis wasn't in work the next day and he'd promised to take Kaitlyn sightseeing, but she was still angry with him from the night before, and when he still hadn't woken up by 11am, she gave up waiting to speak to him and decided to go on her own.

The idea of exploring by herself was terrifying, but her bad mood and the reminder of his friends' words made her determined to prove to Ellis that she was capable of doing things on her own, so she told herself to toughen up, and set off walking.

She went *everywhere*.

First she went to the Empire State Building, going all the way to the top and looking out over the entire city; then she went to Times Square and Central Park where she spent an hour getting lost until she finally managed to find her way out of the other side.

Next she took a taxi to Ground Zero and went around the museum there before walking down Wall Street and along Brooklyn Bridge, taking dozens of pictures whilst she was there.

It was at that point that she began getting phone calls from Ellis but she ignored them all, and instead just sent him a text to say she was fine and was sightseeing on her own.

He messaged back immediately.

Where are you? I'll come and meet you

She didn't reply and just put her phone away, not wanting to let him ruin her day.

When she reached the end of the bridge she briefly explored Brooklyn before booking herself onto a river cruise to go and see the Statue of Liberty.

She found that there were a lot of other solo tourists on the boat so she didn't feel self conscious, and instead just felt proud of herself for managing to explore the entire city on her own.

The only time she felt scared was after the cruise when she walked through the streets of the East village in the dark, and she soon decided that it was probably a good time to go home.

She was starving by that point so she got the taxi to drop her off a few streets away and then went to get herself a chinese take away before strolling the rest of the way to the apartment, wondering if Ellis would be there waiting for her or if he would have gone out with his friends again because he was annoyed about her ignoring his dozens of phone calls.

She put her key in the lock tentatively when she arrived and then jumped back when the door was suddenly pulled open a few seconds later.

She'd expected it would be Ellis who had come to shout at her, but instead it was Angela who stood there.

And she didn't look particularly happy.

Chapter Seventy

"Where on earth have you been?"

Kaitlyn eyed the older women warily, not used to being spoken to in that tone of voice by her.

"I went sightseeing," she said quietly, entering the apartment and finding that Angela seemed to be the only person there. "Where's Ellis?"

"Him and Nicholas have been out for hours trying to look for you."

"But I told him what I was doing!"

"Yes, but when it began to get dark he got worried. He knows how scared you usually are about going out alone here so he was worried you might have gotten lost."

"Oh." Kaitlyn was embarrassed about having caused enough of a fuss that Ellis got his mum and brother involved.

"I'm gonna call them and tell them you're okay," Angela said, pulling out her mobile as Kaitlyn got herself a fork and sat down on the couch to eat her food.

"She's home, Ellis," Angela said into the phone. "She's fine." She listened for a moment. "Okay, see you soon." Hanging up, she announced, "He's on his way back."

"Okay." Kaitlyn gave her a guilty look as the older woman came to sit beside her. "Sorry that you had to get involved in this. I was just angry this morning, and Ellis had promised he'd take me sightseeing, so I decided to go on my own."

"What were you angry about?"

"Didn't Ellis tell you?"

"No, that's why he was so confused about you suddenly going off. I don't think he knows you were mad at him. What happened?"

Kaitlyn told her the story about the night before and how Ellis had basically ignored her the whole time and how his friends had been so rude to her.

Angela sighed. "That doesn't surprise me. I've never liked his friends. Never seen why he hangs out with people like that when he's so different from them."

"Have you said that to him?"

"I did when he was in school after he first started going out with them. But obviously once he got a bit older I knew it wasn't really my place to tell him who he should and shouldn't

249

be friends with." She met Kaitlyn's gaze and gave her a sympathetic look. "I'm sorry, dear. He shouldn't have behaved like that or let his friends tease you. I think I'd be in a mood with him too after that."

Kaitlyn raised her eyebrows pointedly. "Do you see why I disappeared all day now?"

They both laughed.

At that moment, there was a knock on the door and Angela got up saying it must be Nicholas and Tipp. Both men appeared a minute later, with Nicholas looking at Kaitlyn in relief.

"Thank god," he said. "I was worried you might be lost forever."

She scowled at him. "I'm not that useless at finding my way around places."

He gave her a teasing grin and she was pleased he wasn't mad at her, and was back to his usual joking self.

"Oh, by the way, this is Tipp," he said, gesturing to the man at his side. "My boyfriend."

Tipp surprised Kaitlyn by giving her a friendly hug, as if they'd known each other for more than just a few seconds.

"Nicholas has told me a lot about you," he said. "When he told me you'd gone missing I knew I had to come and help look."

"Sorry," she said, blushing.

He grinned widely. "Don't worry about it."

Tipp was very handsome and Kaitlyn couldn't help but be impressed by him. Nicholas had done well.

"Ellis and his stupid friends are to blame for this," Angela told her son.

"What do you mean?"

She and Kaitlyn explained what had happened the night before and Nicholas was soon getting angry on Kaitlyn's behalf.

"He took you out with all those dicks?" he asked, scowling. "I hate those guys! And that's so disrespectful when he's slept with all the girls in that group." He suddenly realised what he'd said and turned to Kaitlyn with guilty eyes. "Shit, sorry. You didn't need to know that."

"It's okay. I'd already figured it out." Hearing her suspicions confirmed however sent a new bolt of anger through her, but she tried not to let it show in front of the others because they were already watching her with pity.

"Well, Ellis deserves this then," Nicholas continued. "If he wants to act like a dick, then he can't expect you to just wait around for him to finally crawl out of bed so you could go out together. I'd have done exactly the same as you."

Kaitlyn smiled at him gratefully.

It was nice to have Ellis's family on her side, even if she did kind of feel bad on him for that; but she felt better about it when she reminded herself that he had been the one to involve them in the first place.

They all looked as if they wanted to shout at him just as much as she did, and when they heard the sound of a key in the lock a few moments later, the four of them all turned towards the entryway with their arms crossed, waiting to confront her boyfriend.

Chapter Seventy One

"Kaitlyn, where the hell did you go?" Ellis asked as he marched into the room before abruptly coming to a halt when he saw the group of people facing him. He eyed them all in confusion. "What's wrong?"

"You didn't tell us that the reason she'd suddenly decided to go off on her own was because you'd upset her," Angela told him.

"What?" Ellis met Kaitlyn's eyes. "What do they mean? Why did I upset you?"

She found it astounding that he didn't already know the issue and that it would have to be explained to him. But, before she could start, Angela spoke again.

"We'll leave you two alone. You probably want to discuss this in private." After collecting her handbag, she gave her son a stern look. "You need to stop spending so much time with those friends of yours, Ellis. They're not good people and Kaitlyn doesn't deserve to have to put up with their rubbish."

Ellis frowned but stayed silent as Nicholas, Angela and Tipp all hugged Kaitlyn and then left with a promise to see them both soon.

After the door had closed behind them, Ellis turned back to Kaitlyn, this time with a guilty look in his eyes.

"So, this is about my friends?"

She scoffed. "How could you not have already guessed that? Did you not see how they treated me last night?"

He shrugged, trying to downplay it all. "They were just joking. They've just got weird sense of humours. But if I'd thought they actually meant what they'd said, I would have defended you."

"You should have defended me anyway," she told him. "But instead you barely acknowledged me all night."

"I was catching up with them! I'm sorry, I didn't mean to ignore you, but I'd just not seen them for so long. I didn't think you'd mind if I didn't give you much attention."

"I felt like a complete outsider! What was the point of taking me out with you if you were just gonna leave me standing on my own for most of the night."

Ellis conceded. "Okay, you're right. I should have just let you stay in and took you out another time."

"Do you think that makes everything better? What about the fact that, not only were they making fun of me all night, which I *don't* believe was a joke, by the way, but I also found out that you apparently used to make fun of me to them!"

At that, Ellis finally looked ashamed, and she got the impression he'd been hoping she had somehow missed that part of his and his friend's conversation.

"It was a long time ago," was his defence. "I'd just moved here and I was still annoyed with you about what you'd said about Nicholas. But I never actually meant any of the things I said."

Kaitlyn didn't believe him. "Are you sure about that? So you don't think I'm weird and plain?"

Ellis sighed and stepped towards her. "Of course I don't." He tried to wrap his arms around her waist but she quickly moved away.

"I didn't like you when you were with them," she told him. "It's like you were a completely different person."

"What do you mean?"

"You seemed so...*fake*. I wasn't sure if that's just how you really are, or if you were putting on a show for them."

Ellis sank down onto the couch and stayed quiet for a few moments. "I don't know what you want me to say. I suppose, yeah I try to impress them a bit. I always have done."

"Why?"

Again, he sighed and then met her eyes, giving her a look as if he was pleading for her to understand. "I told you about how I got teased when we first moved here, right?" Kaitlyn nodded. "Well, when people finally started hanging around with me once they'd heard I'd lost my virginity, I kind of just started acting the same as them because I was worried they wouldn't like me otherwise. And I suppose I never stopped doing that."

Kaitlyn couldn't wrap her head around it. "But why would you want to be friends with them if they didn't like the real you?"

"Because life's different here," he told her. "You don't just make friends based on who your parents know. You have to try and fit in, and if you don't, people will make your life hell."

"Well, that's stupid."

"I know! But it's just the way things are." He reached forward and took her hands. "I'm really sorry for upsetting you, but I swear I didn't mean anything by it. I'm just so used to acting like that around my friends and I didn't even consider your feelings or what you'd think of me."

Kaitlyn understood, but she still didn't agree with it. "Why don't you just find better friends?"

He laughed. "That's what mum's been saying for years. But, I don't know. I'm worried other people won't like me. They always assume English people are boring freaks so they probably wouldn't even give me a chance to show them what I'm really like."

Kaitlyn thought about his words for a moment. "So, basically, if I want your friends to like me I have to act the same way?" He met her eyes, looking sad. "Will I have to start doing that stupid vaping thing?" she asked him. "And taking pictures of myself pulling stupid faces?"

At that, Ellis chuckled. "You make us all sound so pathetic."

She gave him a pointed look and then asked, "If I don't do that, will you be embarrassed of me?"

"No! I could never be embarrassed of you!" He spoke so emphatically. "Look, I promise, if we go out with them again and they start being horrible, I'll tell them all to fuck off and we'll leave."

"Okay," she said quietly.

He cupped her face in his hands. "Do you forgive me for acting like a dick then?"

"Yeah."

He smiled and started to lean towards her for a kiss but she put a hand up to stop him. "But I don't forgive you for taking me out with a bunch of girls you've had sex with, or for letting them openly flirt with you all night."

Chapter Seventy Two

Ellis's throat moved as he swallowed heavily before starting to try and defend himself. "It never meant anything. We've just ended up in bed together a few times when we've been drunk, but it was never more than that. I never dated any of them."

It was just another example of how big the chasm between his and Kaitlyn's lives was. She was starting to worry that it might be insurmountable.

She didn't want to tell him to stop being friends with the girls, but she also didn't know if she could continue to be with him when she would have to deal with them still being a part of his life.

"What are you thinking?" he asked her.

Kaitlyn sighed. "I don't know. I just....I never expected any of this when I decided to move here."

Ellis began to panic. "Are you saying you wished you'd stayed in England?"

"No." She shook her head quickly. "I just thought all the drama would have stopped after my mum. I didn't realise that I'd have to deal with a different kind over here."

He brought his hand up to tangle in her hair, turning her to face him as he stared directly into her eyes. "Kaitlyn, I love you. You know I love you. Don't worry about my friends or those stupid girls. They're not important. All that matters is me and you. Okay?"

Kaitlyn watched him silently, thinking over everything they had discussed and considering how she felt about it all.

Before she had a chance to respond, Ellis swooped forward and latched his mouth onto hers, cradling her face gently as he gave her an enthusiastic kiss.

"Forget about it all, baby," he murmured, pulling back slightly. "Let's just focus on us. Let me show you how much I love you. How much I need you." He gave her another quick kiss. "I'll stop speaking to them all, if that will make you feel better. I'll tell them that everything they've seen from me has been fake, if that's what you want. Just *please* don't be mad at me anymore."

Kailtyn wrapped her arms around his neck. "I'm not mad at you. I love you."

"So, you're not gonna leave me?"

She cracked a smile. "No. I'd have to go and live with my mum again if I did that."

Ellis poked her teasingly. "Thanks. Is that the only reason why you want to stay?"

She gazed into his eyes, seeing everything she wanted in life. "No, I've got a few other reasons."

She placed her mouth back on his.

Chapter Seventy Three

Within moments, Ellis stood up and held out his hand for Kaitlyn to take before they both practically ran towards the bedroom.

She went to move towards the bed but he stopped her and shook his head. "Let's do it here," he told her huskily, pushing her back against the wall and lining his body up with hers so that she was able to feel every inch of him, including the hardness at his hips.

"Here?" Kaitlyn asked in a whisper as Ellis began to kiss her neck and down towards her chest.

He nodded. "I want to bend you over and fuck you from behind. Is that okay?"

She let out a nervous giggle as the space between her legs began to tingle. "Yeah, that's okay."

They undressed each other quickly and then Ellis quickly spun Kaitlyn around so that her back was to him and the side of her face was pressed against the wall as she panted eagerly.

"Stay there," he whispered in her ear before moving away to go and get a condom from his drawer.

He was back a moment later, putting his hands on her hips and positioning her so that she was bent forwards against the wall as she felt him start pushing inside her entrance.

"Fuck, you always feel so good," he graned once he was fully sheathed. "Does it feel good like this baby?"

Kaitlyn could only moan in response. It felt so unbelievably *deep* in that position. It was like his hardness was reaching all the way to her womb.

As Ellis began to move, Kaitlyn did her best to push back against him while also focusing on not losing her balance.

"Oh god," she shouted out involuntarily when he suddenly hit a spot inside her that felt even better than usual.

"That's it baby," he urged her as he started to thrust harder and faster. "I can feel you clenching around me."

"I think I'm gonna..."

"Yes!" he hissed through his clenched teeth. "Come on baby. Come for me."

No further encouragement was needed before Kaitlyn was shaking in ecstasy.

Chapter Seventy Four

"I think we should put you on the pill," Ellis said once they were both laying across the bed, exhausted.

"The what?"

"It's a tablet you take to stop you from getting pregnant," he explained. "It means we wouldn't have to use condoms anymore.

"Oh okay. I've never heard of that before."

"The pill's banned in England," he told her, rolling his eyes. "The government says it's unnatural."

That didn't really surprise Kaitlyn.

Ellis promised to take her to a pharmacy the next day so that she could buy a packet of the strange pills.

"I'll actually wake up this time," he told her jokingly before rolling onto his side to face her. "Speaking of which, tell me about your day of sightseeing."

Kaitlyn smiled as she told him about everywhere she'd gone and everything she'd seen.

"It was amazing," she finished.

"I'm sorry I didn't go with you. I wanted to show you all of that."

"Forget about it," she said, stroking his cheek. "It was actually good for me to go out on my own and see that I'm not completely useless at doing things by myself. Maybe I'll actually fit in around here eventually."

Ellis smiled and tucked some of her hair behind her ear. "It doesn't matter if you don't," he told her softly. "I like that you're not the same as everyone else. I've always liked that about you, even when we were kids. I mean, yeah sometimes you had the same opinions as your mum because you'd been taught to think like that, but underneath it all I've always known you were your own person. I never want you to change that."

Kaitlyn smiled. "I won't."

He suddenly reached across her to open the top drawer of his bedside table, pulling out a silver locket on a black cord which could obviously be worn as a necklace.

"Here you go."

"What's this?"

"Open it."

Kaitlyn frowned but pulled on the clasp to reveal that there was a picture of the two of them as kids inside. From how they looked, she guessed it must have been taken shortly before Ellis and his family left England.

"How long have you had this?" she asked him.

"Years. I made it not long after we got here. I used to wear it all the time but then my neck got too fat so I just left it in my drawer."

Kaitlyn laughed. "So why are you showing me this now?"

His hand slid from her bare bottom, over her hips and up to her naked chest where he then traced her tattoo with his forefinger. "Because I want you to know I've never been embarrassed of you. I never could be. You're everything to me, and you always have been. Even when we were apart all those years. I always knew that, even if I never saw you again, anyone else I met would just be second best."

Kaitlyn had tears in her eyes by the time he finished speaking. She knew she should say something equally as special, but she had never been particularly good with words, so instead she lifted the necklace and placed it over her head so that the locket fell just above her breasts.

He watched her with a smile on his face which soon disappeared when she moved to straddle his lap, cupping his face between her hands and staring down at him intently.

"Make love to me, Ellis."

The End